GENIE
IN TROUBLE

Ciaran Murtagh is a writer and actor. His first book, *Dinopants*, was published by Piccadilly Press and was followed by three sequels. He also writes TV shows and has recently been involved with scripting *The Slammer*, *The 4 O'Clock Club*, *Diddy Movies*, *The Legend of Dick and Dom*, *Scoop*, *Hotel Trubble*, and *Dennis and Gnasher*. He regularly appears in TV shows for CBBC and can be seen in every series of *The Slammer* and in *Dick and Dom's Hoopla*.

He lives in London with his wife and secret sweetie cupboard and has a lovely daughter called Eleanor. He is an unapologetic fan of the music of a-ha and still sucks his thumb. It is unclear which of these two facts is more embarrassing to his friends and family.

Find out more at www.ciaranmurtagh.com

Also in the *Genie* series:
Genie in Training

Other books by Ciaran Murtagh:

Dinopants
Dinopoo
Dinoburps
Dinoball

CIARAN MURTAGH

GENIE IN TROUBLE

Illustrated by
Adria Meserve

Piccadilly Press • London

For Dylan the dude and Rose the dudette
– may all your teapots
be filled with genies.

First published in Great Britain in 2012
by Piccadilly Press Ltd,
5 Castle Road, London NW1 8PR
www.piccadillypress.co.uk

A catalogue record for this book is available
from the British Library

ISBN: 978 1 84812 279 6 (paperback)

1 3 5 7 9 10 8 6 4 2

Printed in the UK by CPI Group (UK), Croydon, CR0 4TD
Cover design by Simon Davis
Cover and interior illustrations by Adria Meserve

CHAPTER 1

Jamie Quinn raced through the school gates. His heart was pounding and he was gasping for breath – he'd run all the way from his house without stopping because he was so desperate to show Dylan Reid, his best friend and sweet sharer, what was in his rucksack. Surely Dylan would *have* to believe him now.

Jamie screeched to a halt and scoured the

playground. Dylan was clambering up the climbing frame trying to get away from his gran. She was determined to give him a particularly squelchy goodbye kiss and he was having none of it! Jamie smiled as he watched Dylan swing across the monkey bars and escape down the slide.

When Dylan saw Jamie, he ran over. 'Thank goodness you're here,' he said, rummaging in his bag for his robo-bugs. 'She's getting worse! Time for a bug battle before class?' Dylan didn't wait for an answer and popped the bugs on the ground. 'Do you want to be the blue destroyer or the red devil?'

Jamie loved robo-bugs, but wasn't in the mood for playing today. He shrugged off his rucksack and tugged at the zip.

'I've got the teapot,' said Jamie. 'The one the genie was trapped in.' Dylan rolled his eyes. 'Not this again! You've been going on about genies for three days!

You're giving me the genie jitters! If you're not careful *I* might disappear in a puff of smoke!'

Jamie took out the battered old teapot and handed it to Dylan.

'You seriously expect me to believe there was a genie living in this?' said Dylan, peering down the spout. 'What was he? Typhoo or PG Tips?'

Jamie rolled his eyes. 'His name was Balthazar Najar, and he took me to the Genie Academy in Lampville-upon-Cloud where I learnt to be a genie. I spent a whole term there but —'

'But you were only away for a night here because time moves quicker up there. You told me,' interrupted Dylan. 'And you can't do genie magic here, which is a shame because I have an older sister who could do with being turned into a frog! It wouldn't be hard, she's halfway there already.' Dylan was starting to worry about his friend. Jamie was normally fairly sensible, but ever since Jamie's dotty old gran had given him a teapot for his birthday, he'd been going on about academies and wishes and magic all the time.

Dylan prised off the lid and examined the

inside of the teapot closely. 'It looks empty to me,' he said, handing it back.

'It is *now*,' explained Jamie patiently. 'The genie flew out when I rubbed the teapot with my sweaty football sock.'

'I don't blame him,' Dylan said, laughing. 'One of your pongy football socks is enough to send anyone flying! Why was a genie living in a teapot, anyway? Don't they live in lamps?'

'I already told you,' said Jamie, stuffing the teapot back into his rucksack. 'Genies normally live in the clouds. They only get put in lamps when they do something wrong. If they do something wrong a second time, they get put in a teapot and if they do something wrong again, they get banished to a bottle at the bottom of the sea.'

'Of course they do,' said Dylan, arching an eyebrow. 'And then King Neptune pokes them with his trident while a mermaid sings a song about trousers!'

'Fine!' huffed Jamie. 'Don't believe me!'

Dylan gave his friend a reassuring squeeze on the arm. 'I think you just had one of those really good dreams that seem real even when you wake up.'

'I *wasn't* dreaming,' said Jamie grumpily.

Just then the school bell rang. It was time for lessons.

'I won't believe you until I see a real genie,' said Dylan. 'One who grants wishes and everything. Until that happens, I reckon you're as mad as a gerbil on a trampoline!'

Jamie sighed. No genie was ever just going to appear out of thin air at school.

But right at that moment, in the shadows on the far side of the playground, there was a flash of light and a puff of smoke. A figure wearing a black waistcoat and a pair of black pantaloons appeared among the trees. The figure watched unseen as the two boys trudged into the school. He'd found Jamie Quinn at last.

CHAPTER 2

Jamie didn't really blame Dylan for thinking he was mad. Perhaps he shouldn't have told him about making food out of clouds, or about the flying paintbrushes, and playing basketball ten metres off the ground riding on a genie's back. And he definitely shouldn't have mentioned the magic carpet racing. He unzipped his pencil case, which was covered in racing cars, and took out his favourite pencil. Jamie smiled as he remembered how Balthazar had granted his wish to become a racing car driver. He'd whizzed and zoomed around a racetrack, and even won the race – it had been brilliant!

'Surprise spelling test,' announced Miss Rothwell from the front of the class.

Jamie's heart sank and his memory popped like a bubble. He *hated* spelling tests.

'Spelling one,' she trilled. '*Dandelion*.'

As the rest of the class began to write, Jamie stared at the page in front of him and sighed. In the Genie Academy there had been no such thing as a boring lesson. Snake charming, wish granting, lamp squeezing . . . Even lessons that sounded rubbish were amazing. Jamie had thought that lamp polishing would be the worst lesson ever until he started scrubbing – fireworks had shot from every lamp he'd touched and the classroom had been filled with whizzes, bangs and crashes. The teacher had magicked up five big fans to get rid of the smoke and two genies had nearly been blown out of the window.

Just then, there was a small flash of light by his pencil case. Jamie looked down and his mouth dropped open in shock. Standing next to it was the unmistakable figure of Balthazar Najar – his genie friend – but he had shrunk to the size of Jamie's thumb. He was grinning and waving.

Jamie rubbed his eyes – then looked again. The genie was still there! Jamie was so shocked he fell off his chair.

'Are you all right, Jamie?' asked Miss Rothwell.

'Erm, I'm just excited because I love spelling so much,' said Jamie, dusting himself down.

'Really?' said Miss Rothwell. 'Well, try to contain yourself a little longer – we're only on question two. Spell *bamboozle*.'

Jamie settled back in his chair and stared at the place where Balthazar had been, but the little genie had disappeared.

Just as Jamie began to write, there was another flash, and this time Balthazar appeared on the end of his pencil, riding it like a cowboy would ride a bucking bronco. He was obviously trying to say something, but his voice was too tiny to be heard.

Balthazar was clinging on tightly, but he suddenly lost his grip and pinged into the air like a big black bogey. He landed on Jamie's shoulder. 'There's trouble in Lampville!' the tinny voice yelled.

'Not now,' whispered Jamie, swatting Balthazar away. 'I'm in the middle of a test!'

'No, you've got to come with me – right away!' squeaked Balthazar, flying into Jamie's shirt pocket and tickling his armpit.

Jamie wriggled in his seat and prodded Balthazar with his finger, but he dodged out of the way and zoomed straight up Jamie's nose to take cover.

'Get out of there!' gasped Jamie.

Balthazar stuck his head out. 'It's disgusting up here, Jamie. When did you last blow your nose?'

Jamie poked at his itchy nose with a finger.

'Jamie Quinn!' shouted Miss Rothwell. 'Stop picking your nose! Go and get a tissue from the toilet this instant!'

Jamie hurried from the room, his face red as the class giggled behind him.

As soon as he got to the boys' toilets, Balthazar emerged from his nose. 'Shan't be a sec!' squeaked the mini genie as he closed his eyes and blew a wish. His breath sparkled and Balthazar was covered in the shimmering cloud. The sound of rushing wind filled the room and Jamie watched in amazement as Balthazar's arms zoomed back to their normal size. Their weight made Balthazar's tiny body topple forward.

'Oops!' squeaked the genie as his nose hit the

floor. 'I really should practise this!'

Balthazar's legs began to grow and soon, with his tiny body and four long limbs, he looked like an angry daddy long legs. Jamie laughed. It seemed like Balthazar was just as bad at wish granting as ever!

'This should do it!' squeaked Balthazar again. The genie closed his eyes and held his breath and his body began to expand as if he'd eaten nothing but fish and chips for a week!

'How do I look?' he asked when he'd finished. 'Handsome as ever?'

Jamie pointed at Balthazar's ears. They were still tiny. 'I think you forgot something,' he said.

'What's that? Speak up! I can't hear you,' said Balthazar.

Jamie pointed to his ears. Balthazar looked in a mirror, shrieked, and popped his ears back to their normal size. 'Better?'

'Back to their pointy best!' laughed Jamie. Genies' ears were always pointy – it was one of the main ways you could tell genies apart from humans.

'It's good to see you again, Jamie Najar,' said Balthazar, using Jamie's genie clan name.

'It's good to see you too,' said Jamie, giving Balthazar a hug. 'But you could have waited until break-time. Everyone thinks I've gone bananas!'

'It couldn't wait, Jamie,' said Balthazar, suddenly losing his smile. 'Awful things are happening in Lampville. Terrible, terrible things!'

'But I've only been gone three days!' said Jamie.

'Three days of your time is much longer in genie time, remember,' said Balthazar. 'It's been almost a year. You need to come back – you're our only hope.'

Balthazar's voice cracked and, for the first time, Jamie looked at his friend properly. There were lines across his forehead that hadn't been there before. It looked like Balthazar hadn't slept a wink in months. And why was he wearing a black waistcoat rather than the usual Najar red? 'What's happened?' asked Jamie.

Balthazar took Jamie's hands in his. 'You need to see for yourself,' he said quietly, 'but I'm not allowed to just take a human into the genie world. Make a wish to go back to the Academy and I'll grant it. Hurry!'

Jamie knew for certain that whatever was going on in Lampville was very bad indeed. Balthazar was never this serious. If Balthazar thought Jamie could help, he wanted to try. He closed his eyes. 'I wish to be back at the Genie Academy,' he said.

Balthazar clapped his hands in delight. 'Easy peezy, lemon squeezy! Nothing's hard if you're a

genie!' he sang, blowing a
shimmering, sparkling breath
towards Jamie.

Jamie felt Balthazar's breath
flow over him, then he had
the familiar tickly
feeling in his
stomach.

He opened his eyes to see a flash of light, and
the room filled with starry smoke. Jamie felt wind
rush through his hair as his feet lifted from the
ground. He was excited to be going back to the
Academy – surely nothing too awful could be
happening in such a magical world?

CHAPTER 3

When the smoke cleared, Jamie was standing by the tall gates of the Genie Academy. The mighty Academy building towered above him, its turrets rising majestically into the sky. Like all of the buildings in the genie world, it was made from clouds which had solidified over time.

Through the gates, Jamie saw some of the trainee genies hard at work in the beautiful gardens. Spades and pitchforks hovered in mid-air,

controlled by
genie magic,
and a
wheelbarrow
loaded with
clouds flew
past and emptied

itself on a cloud heap in the corner. Jamie shook his head – he'd never totally understand the genie world. They could magic up some things, like food, but they still had to do boring things like gardening and cleaning! Balthazar had once explained that most genie wishes only lasted a short time – if genies wanted something to last, they still had to do it the hard way. Jamie tried to spot any familiar faces and grinned when he recognised the unmistakable shaggy yellow-haired back of Adeel Maloof's head. During Jamie's term at the Academy, Adeel had been his best school friend. 'Adeel!' shouted Jamie

as he started to run to the gates.
Balthazar shrieked, grabbed
Jamie by the shoulder
and quickly pulled him

behind a bush, just as Adeel turned round.

'Things have changed, Jamie,' hissed Balthazar. 'You can't show everyone that you're here. I trust Adeel, of course, but who else would have heard you?! You in particular must be very careful.'

What did Balthazar mean? Jamie peeked out from the bush. He suddenly realised that all of the genies were wearing black waistcoats – just like Balthazar. That wasn't right. When he was last there, the genies wore a different coloured waistcoat depending on what clan they belonged to. The Kassabs wore green, the Ganims blue, Balthazar wore red because he was a Najar – Jamie too because Balthazar had brought him to the Academy – and Adeel should have been wearing yellow because he was a Maloof.

'Why is everyone wearing black?' Jamie asked.

'The clans and their colours have been abolished,' said Balthazar quietly.

Jamie gasped. 'Why would the Genie Congress do that? I'm shocked Methuzular would allow it in his school.'

'Methuzular isn't headmaster of the Academy any more,' said Balthazar sadly. 'That job belongs to Dakhil Ganim.'

'No!' spluttered Jamie. Dakhil Ganim was one of the nastiest genies Jamie had met. He was ruthless and mean – everything that wise, kind Methuzular was not. And Dakhil's son, Dabir, had once trapped Jamie inside a magic lamp. If Dakhil had such an important job, things in the genie world must be bad.

Balthazar pointed to the sign above the school gates. For thousands of years it had proudly displayed the genie motto, *Live lightly and shine brightly*, but now it had been smeared with thick black paint and read, *Be the best and beat the rest*.

Just then they saw a genie with a long silver sword making his way along the other side of the gate.

'One of Dakhil's guards,' hissed Balthazar. 'Another new thing about the Academy. If he spots you, we'll be in for it – we need to get away from here!'

Keeping low to the ground, Balthazar led Jamie behind a cloud hedgerow, through a narrow gap in the fence, and down an overgrown path towards a rickety shed.

'We'll be safe in here,' said Balthazar, taking Jamie inside and wiping some dust off a creaky cloud chair for Jamie to sit in. 'Home sweet home!' he said, spreading his arms and knocking over a paint tin. 'It's the storage shed where I keep my cleaning equipment. No one comes here apart from me.' Balthazar rapped his knuckles proudly on a shelf. It came away from the wall and bottles of cleaner and polish toppled onto the floor. He kicked them behind a curtain.

Jamie rolled his eyes. Balthazar was just as accident-prone as ever.

'I'm still the caretaker's assistant at the Academy. I think Dakhil wants to keep me close by – he's never liked me, and I think he's hoping I'll give him a reason to banish me to a bottle at the bottom of the sea.'

Jamie shuddered at the thought. Genies could be banished if they broke a rule in the Genie Code:

Rule one:
Do not steal from another genie.

Rule two:
Do not use your wishes for evil.

Rule three:
Never back down from a genie challenge.

☆ Rule four:
Always obey your master when tied to
a lamp, teapot or bottle.

☆ Rule five:
Grant every wish your master asks.

The last rule was the one that Balthazar struggled with; he didn't always get his wishes quite right. He did his best but was easily confused. Once he'd made a man fart for a whole week because he'd wished he had wind power in his house. Balthazar was easily distracted too, and when he was training at the Academy himself, he'd turned the Mayor of London into a Rice Krispie. It was those kind of mistakes that had led to Balthazar's banishment into the teapot that Jamie's gran had given him for his birthday. If Balthazar made another mistake and broke the Genie Code again, he would be banished to a bottle at the bottom of the sea, where it was likely he would never be released. Jamie knew Balthazar was terrified this might happen.

Balthazar clapped his hands and tried to smile.

'Anyway, it's good to see you Jamie. Who's for some biscuits?' Without waiting for a reply, he scooped up some cloud from the floor, inhaled deeply and blew out a wish. When the sparkles cleared, the cloud had been transformed into a plate piled high with chocolate biscuits. In the genie world, you could eat whatever you wished for.

Jamie wondered if his magical powers might work now he was back in Lampville. He scooped up some cloud, breathed in deeply, held his breath until he felt his mind click into the right place for magic,

 and then blew out a wish of his own, transforming the cloud into two bowls of ice cream. 'You haven't forgotten that, I see!' said Balthazar, taking a chocolate biscuit and dipping it in the ice cream. As he tried to propel the huge scoop into his mouth, a big dollop of ice cream splattered onto his waistcoat. 'A treat for later!' he giggled.

Suddenly they heard footsteps. Someone was approaching the shed!

'The guard must have seen you and followed us here!' Balthazar said, snatching the bowl from Jamie's hands and hiding it behind some dusters. He dragged Jamie towards a rickety cupboard. 'Hide!' he hissed.

As the door to the shed began to open, Jamie squeezed inside the cupboard. Balthazar pulled some overalls in front of him, and quickly threw himself into the cloud chair, trying to look innocent.

'Balthazar, are you there?' whispered a familiar voice. 'It's me – Adeel.'

Jamie breathed a sigh of relief, came out of his hiding place and gave his friend a huge hug.

'Adeel!' he said. 'You nearly gave us heart attacks.'

'I knew you were back!' said Adeel. 'I recognised your voice when you called me. I tried to work out where you would have gone and figured you must be with Balthazar. Nice plunger, by the way! Is it a new human fashion?'

Jamie looked in a dusty mirror. He had a plunger on his head. He looked like a bumper car. It must have fallen on him while he was in the cupboard.

Jamie took the plunger off his head and sat back

down. He was desperate to know what had happened since he'd been away, and asked his genie friend to tell him all about it.

'Well, I can do a transformation wish now. Watch this!' Adeel inhaled deeply and wished that he was a bright yellow parrot. 'Cool, huh?' he chirped as he swooped around the little shed.

Jamie was very impressed even though the space was so small that Adeel kept crashing into the walls.

'Of course all that stopped when Dakhil took over,' said Adeel, transforming himself back to normal. 'We don't have any wish lessons now. And we've got guards who patrol everywhere and stop us from doing any wishes for fun. They can't even be bothered to wish up their own dinner – I have to wish it up for them every evening and take it to them.'

'You always did make the best fig burgers,' said Jamie.

'What about you?' Adeel asked. 'What are you doing here?'

'He's here to save us all,' said Balthazar.

Jamie almost fell off his chair. 'I'm *what*?!'

CHAPTER 4

'Let me explain,' said Balthazar gently. 'Dakhil has never liked humans. Dakhil's father, Dimar, wasn't a skilful genie – he kept getting things wrong, but everyone suspected he did it on purpose. He was often given the benefit of the doubt, but did get banished twice. One day a human wished for a bit of peace and quiet and Dimar wished away his ears. Dimar knew what he had done was wrong but he didn't care. He was about to be banished to a bottle at the bottom of the sea for his meanness, when Dimar used a wish to make himself disappear.'

'Where did he go?' asked Jamie.

'Nobody knows,' said Balthazar, shrugging his shoulders. 'Nobody had ever managed to do it before. Dakhil was just a little boy, and was teased and taunted for years. The shadow of his father's cowardice hung over him all through the Academy. But instead of blaming his father, he blamed humans. "If we didn't have to grant their wishes when they find us in lamps, teapots and bottles," he would grumble, "and look after them the rest of the time to stop them getting into trouble, then my dad would still be here!" Dakhil has vowed revenge ever since.'

Jamie shook his head. It was a sad story.

'Dakhil worked hard to get the power he now has,' continued Balthazar. 'He started spreading rumours about Methuzular at the Genie Congress – which he's head of, as you know. He said that Methuzular was a traitor and that he was going to betray us all by telling humans about the genie world – and that letting you into the Academy,

Jamie, was the first part of his evil plan to help humans infiltrate Lampville and take us over. Genies know that if humans find out about them, they will start relying on genies all the time. We'd be rushed off our feet!

'Anyway,' Balthazar went on, 'late one night, I was doing some extra cleaning in Methuzular's office. I'd, um, accidentally made his dustbin explode.'

'I remember that,' said Adeel. 'You promised to make your cleaning go with a bang!'

'It kind of worked,' Balthazar muttered. 'I'd promised Methuzular it would be cleared up by morning. I was just getting the banana skin off the lampshade when I heard Dakhil and Methuzular arguing outside. I hid behind the cloak stand and watched as Dakhil dragged Methuzular into the office and had him surrounded by guards. They forced Methuzular to write a letter to you, Jamie.'

'To me?' said Jamie, surprised.

'Dakhil dictated it for Methuzular to write down,' Balthazar continued, 'so it would be in his handwriting. It said that everything was going to plan. Soon humans would know all about genies and before long genies would be nothing more than wish-granting pets! He said he was coming to stay with you while he organised a human invasion.'

Jamie gasped. 'But that's just not true!'

'That's what Methuzular said, but Dakhil said that unless he wrote the letter and signed it, then they'd destroy the Academy brick by brick.'

'Methuzular would do anything to protect the Academy,' said Adeel.

Balthazar nodded. 'Dakhil knew that, and so Methuzular signed the letter. His reputation might have been ruined, but at least the Academy would be saved.'

'What have they done with him?' asked Jamie.

'I heard Dakhil tell his guards to take him to Lampville Jail,' said Balthazar, shuddering.

'I knew it couldn't be true!' said Adeel. 'But most people think he's abandoned the genie world and gone to live with you, Jamie. That's why they agreed Dakhil should be headmaster of the Academy.' Adeel looked down at the ground. 'He made everyone wear black, rather than bright colours. Not just here in the Academy but across the whole genie world. He convinced the Genie Congress that genies should be united as one against the human threat and there was no need for clans at this time of approaching war. The Genie Congress agreed, then he was allowed to change Academy lessons too. As most wishes only last for a little while, and we'd eventually get tired in a long fight, he said we had to be able to fight the humans in other ways. So now we do lots of physical work to build our muscles and we practise using swords and ropes. He says nothing beats exercise and practice if we want to be ready for when the humans attack.'

'But there won't be an attack,' said Jamie.

'*We* know that, Jamie,' said Balthazar, 'but the other genies can't be sure. They all heard about you coming to the Academy, and I couldn't tell anyone what I knew in case Dakhil found out and sent me to jail – or the bottle. Not all genies like what Dakhil is doing, but they're just too scared to admit it to each other . . . Especially now. As headmaster of the Academy, Dakhil has the Book of Wishes – the most powerful book in the genie world.'

Jamie remembered the dusty old book that had once sat on Methuzular's bookcase. It contained the guiding words you spoke in your head for every wish genies had ever made. The thought that Dakhil had such power filled Jamie with fear.

'Dakhil has spies everywhere,' said Balthazar. 'Nobody trusts anyone any more. Genies who stand up to Dakhil just disappear. You're our only hope.'

'But what can I do against someone as powerful as Dakhil?' spluttered Jamie.

'I thought you could speak to the Genie Congress,' said Balthazar. 'You could tell them there is no plan, that the humans aren't up to anything.'

Jamie shook his head. 'If they don't trust a genie

as wise and powerful as Methuzular, they're certainly not going to trust me. Dakhil is head of the Genie Congress, don't forget. Telling them there is no plan is exactly what they'd expect me to say, isn't it?'

Adeel bit his lip. 'Jamie's right,' he admitted, turning to Balthazar. 'You should speak to them. Tell them everything you've seen and heard.'

Balthazar's eyes grew wide. 'There's more chance of me turning blue and dancing the can-can than there is of Dakhil letting me speak to the Congress!' he said.

'Then go into town and tell all the genies there,' suggested Jamie.

Balthazar shook his head frantically. 'Nobody listens to a word I say any more. I've made too many mistakes to be taken seriously. They'd just say I'd got the wrong end of the stick, as usual.'

They sat in silence for a moment, the size of the problem weighing heavy on their shoulders.

'If only Methuzular were here,' said Jamie. 'He'd know what to do.'

Balthazar looked up suddenly. 'That's it!' he said,

clicking his fingers in triumph. 'We need to find a way to speak to Methuzular.'

'But that's impossible!' Adeel said. 'Methuzular's in jail. And no one's ever managed to break out of Lampville Jail. It's trickier than a magician who's just got out of trick school with a new box of tricks marked *Tricky*.'

Balthazar grinned. 'But we don't need him to break *out*. We just need to break *in*. We only need to talk to him. Well, not *we*, exactly . . .' He caught Jamie's eye. 'You want *me* to break into Lampville Jail?' Jamie gasped. 'Dakhil would notice if Adeel or

I went missing,' said Balthazar, 'but nobody else knows you're here.'

'Hang on!' said Jamie. 'If I get caught then I'm done for! Dakhil will lock me up and I'll never see the light of day – or another episode of *Top Gear* – again.'

'Then don't get caught,' said Balthazar.

Suddenly a loud gong rang outside and Balthazar and Adeel jumped to attention.

'Lesson time,' said Adeel, running to the door.

'And I have to clean the canteen,' said Balthazar.

Before he left, Balthazar turned to Jamie. 'You have to speak to Methuzular, Jamie,' he pleaded. 'You must find a way. Please. But be careful! Trust no one and try not to think about the terrible punishment Dakhil will dream up if you get caught. He'd probably turn you into a rhino's bum wart or something.'

'You're not helping!' snapped Jamie as Balthazar and Adeel darted through the shed door. Suddenly a spelling test with Miss Rothwell didn't seem so bad after all.

CHAPTER 5

Jamie sat on the cloud chair, thinking hard. First he had to get to the centre of Lampville without being spotted, then he had to break into a heavily guarded prison. Even if he got that far, he would have to make his way through a prison which was presumably full of rogues and scoundrels, without getting torn to pieces, to find the one person nobody was supposed to know was there. It really was impossible.

A bowl of melting ice-cream caught his eye. Not long ago he had thought that wishes and genies were impossible too, and how wrong he had been! He had to at least try – Balthazar, Adeel and every good genie in the genie world were counting on him.

Jamie looked at his human clothes. He wouldn't get very far dressed in his school uniform, or in a wished set of clothes that would fade after a short while. The least Balthazar could have done was get him a black genie outfit to match everybody else's.

He searched the storeroom for a disguise and his eyes came to rest on a baggy bright purple boilersuit hanging in the cupboard. Jamie changed out of his uniform and wrinkled his nose as he pulled on the dusty boilersuit. He might look like

a massive blackberry but it was better than what he had been wearing. Hopefully everyone would just assume he was a caretaker.

He crept out of the storeroom and slipped out of the school grounds using Balthazar's secret path to reach the road to Lampville. He could see the genie town sprawling in the distance like a miniature marshmallow city. The sun was low in the sky and long shadows stretched from the cloud trees all along the road to Lampville. Jamie stuck

to the shade as if his life depended on it. Which, he thought, it really might.

There were not many genies on the road at that time of day, and eventually Jamie reached the outskirts of the city. He hid behind a wall and took in his surroundings. Tall houses lined both sides of the street, which was bustling with genies. It was just as he'd remembered it, except now every single genie was wearing black. Jamie realised that he really needed to find an alternative to the bright purple boilersuit – it made him stand out like a sore thumb.

Jamie watched a plump genie hang her washing on a line nearby. A black waistcoat and pantaloons that looked his size fluttered temptingly in the breeze. He only needed to borrow them . . . They might be a bit soggy but they would do.

He was about to make his move when a little boy spotted him crouching behind the wall. 'Are you playing hide and seek?' he asked. 'Can I play too?'

Jamie put his fingers to his lips to try and shush the boy but he was already making his way over.

'What are you wearing?' he asked. 'You've got funny ears. Is it fancy dress?'

The little genie began to giggle and poked Jamie's ears with a sticky finger.

Just then the boy's mother noticed he was gone and started to look for him. When she saw him standing by Jamie, she stared at him intently. Then she screamed. 'A human! There's a human trying to steal my baby!'

Jamie couldn't believe his bad luck. She must have seen his non-pointy ears!

A few others genies turned round. Jamie thought about trying to explain the truth, but they were already crowding round him, and they did not look happy.

He didn't wait to find out what they would do – he leapt up and dodged past the genies like a striker in a football match, running fast down the road – but they gave chase. When Jamie glanced over his shoulder, he could see six angry genies were gaining on him fast.

Jamie darted down a narrow alley, which led to a courtyard filled with shops and restaurants. He splashed straight through the magnificent fountain in the middle, and raced towards the road on the other side. As he hurtled past the back entrance of a café, Jamie spotted a huge rubbish bin standing just outside the door and lifted the lid. The bin was full of food scraps, but Jamie didn't care – well, he did, but it was better than being caught. He held his nose and jumped inside, pulling the lid down after him. Outside, he could hear the cries and shouts of the pursuing genies but nobody seemed to know where he had gone.

Minutes crawled by like hours. Jamie tried to stay still as something brown and sticky dripped on his shoulder and his foot got pricked by a fish bone. The bin smelt worse than one of his baby brother's nappies on curry day.

When he dared to raise the lid to take a peek, night had fallen and flaming torches now lit the streets. Jamie climbed out of the bin, wondering how he could move around without being seen. A pile of boxes caught his eye. He scampered up them and onto the roof of the café. All the genie buildings were close together, and he was able to creep from rooftop to rooftop like a big purple ninja, all the way to the Grand Bazaar.

The Grand Bazaar was a magnificent square, the size of two football pitches, at the very heart of the town. Jamie dodged through the darkness and found that one of the clothes shops he'd remembered from his previous visit was still open. A tall, skinny genie was packing away her wares. Jamie watched as she lifted down racks of black waistcoats and pantaloons with a long pole. A sign above the door read *Ivana Waistcoat's Clothes Shop*.

Ivana carried the waistcoats into the shop and Jamie realised this was his chance. Ivana wouldn't miss one waistcoat, would she? He climbed down a pipe and sneaked over to the shopfront, stood on his tiptoes and lifted one down. As his fingers closed around the black silk, a heavy hand grabbed his shoulder.

'What do you think you're doing?' Ivana shouted. 'I'm going to have you arrested this instant! Guards! Guards!'

Just then a plump little genie came out of the shop to see what all the commotion was about. Jamie recognised her instantly as Aunty Fadiyah, the genie that ran the uniform store in the Academy.

'What's going on?' she demanded. Then she saw Jamie. 'Jamie Najar? What are you doing here?' she said, giving him a big hug and then wrinkling her nose. 'And why do you smell like fish farts?'

'You know this boy?' asked Ivana, confused.

Fadiyah nodded. 'He was the human who came to the Academy,' she explained.

'A human!' bellowed Ivana, horrified. 'So they were right! The invasion has started! Guards! Guards!'

Fadiyah quickly put a hand over Ivana's mouth and pulled her into the shop. 'Calm down, sister, dear. Jamie was always a good boy, and I told you this invasion business was nonsense. Methuzular wouldn't sell out the genies any more than you'd sell out of waistcoats!'

Ivana's eyes bulged.

'You'd better let her go,' said Jamie, following them in. 'I don't think she can breathe!'

'Given how you smell, Jamie, lucky her!' said Fadiyah, taking her hand away.

Ivana gasped for air and fixed her sister with a fierce stare. 'You'd better know what you're doing,' she spluttered.

Jamie didn't know what to say. Balthazar had made it clear he should trust no one, but he'd grown fond of Fadiyah in the Academy; she'd never been angry when he had to keep popping back for a new uniform after singeing, tearing or blowing up bits of his clothes while he was learning to grant wishes. She had said that she still trusted Methuzular, too. He was sure she would believe him, but would her sister? Jamie thought he had little choice but to risk it.

While Ivana squirted him with some of her perfume, he repeated everything he had heard from Balthazar — the conversation he'd overheard with Methuzular and the guards, the fake letter and the fact that Methuzular hadn't run away, but instead was locked up in Lampville Jail.

Ivana and Fadiyah were silent throughout.

'I knew that Dakhil was up to no good,' said Ivana eventually.

'Your story makes a lot more sense than Methuzular betraying the genies,' agreed Fadiyah.

Jamie breathed a sigh of relief. At least they believed him. 'So,' he said, 'I'm going to try to break into the jail and speak to Methuzular. We hope he might know how we can defeat Dakhil.'

'Well, I don't think anyone's ever tried to break *in* to Lampville Jail before,' said Ivana, thoughtfully. 'At least no one will be expecting that. Maybe we can help.'

She made her way to the back of the shop and began to rummage in a box, eventually holding up a blue and gold striped waistcoat with matching pantaloons and hat.

'A prison guard uniform,' said Fadiyah triumphantly. 'We make them! What better way to break in to a jail than disguised as a guard?'

Jamie gave Ivana and Fadiyah a grin. They might just have come up with the perfect plan. But his smile quickly faded as he realised this only meant that things were about to get very dangerous indeed.

CHAPTER 6

Ivana and Fadiyah insisted that Jamie spend the night in their home above the shop – once he'd agreed to have a bath; it was too late for anyone to be walking the streets of Lampville on their own, even if they were dressed as a prison guard.

They clucked around him like two mother hens on egg-hatching day and after a reassuringly ordinary dinner of sausages and mashed potato wished up by Ivana, Jamie was so tired that he slept soundly on the soft cloud bed.

The next morning, Ivana helped Jamie into the uniform. It was a little bit big but Fadiyah made some quick alterations. 'I can't do anything about the hat, I'm afraid,' she said, popping a big blue fez on Jamie's head.

Jamie felt the fez slide down. 'At least it covers my ears! But don't I look a bit young to be a prison guard?'

'Good point,' admitted Fadiyah, stroking her chin. Suddenly she clicked her fingers. 'Why don't you tell them it's a new lesson Dakhil's come up with? He wants students at the Academy to spend some time learning to be prison guards so they'll grow up to be tough like him.'

'It sounds like the sort of thing he'd say,' agreed Ivana.

Ivana and Fadiyah showed Jamie out through the back of the shop into an alley behind the Grand Bazaar. 'Turn left at Joanna Teacosy's place and go straight past Cloud Hall,' Ivana said. 'Lampville Jail is just a bit further on. It's the only building made of thunderclouds – you can't miss it.'

'Thank you,' said Jamie with a warm smile. 'You've been ever so kind.'

As Jamie made his way to the prison, he noticed people stopping and backing away from him. At first he worried it was because they could see his human ears or were wondering why someone so young was dressed as a guard, but then Jamie realised that the genies were scared of him.

Lampville Jail was unmistakable. It was a tall, grey building made of angry clouds, which flickered with lightning, and stood on its own in the middle of the street like a dirty smudge. Jamie felt a shiver run down his spine. Could he really get away with this? He remembered what Ivana had told him: 'Be confident, and you can get away with more than you would imagine.'

Jamie was about to knock on the large grey door when a small shutter slid back and a pair of dark eyes peered out at him. 'Whaddya want?' barked a voice.

Jamie's heart began to thump. A lump came to his throat and his mouth went dry. He couldn't find the words to speak even if he had known what to say.

'Well?' said the voice again. 'I haven't got all day.'

Jamie was about to turn and run when he remembered playing the part of the nasty baddie Willy Killme in the school play at Christmas. Miss Rothwell had taught him to clench his teeth before he spoke and to make his shoulders big and square. It had worked in the play — maybe it would work now. It was worth trying.

'Dakhil sent me,' he replied, puffing himself up. 'He wants pupils at the Academy to spend some time helping out in the prison. He says it'll make us tougher.'

'He's got a point,' sneered the voice. 'You kids are so wimpy that every time you hear a thunder crack you wish up beds to hide under. He could have warned me though.'

The shutter slid into place and the door swung open. A mean-looking genie with three black teeth and a grey stubbly beard peered down at him. He was wearing the same uniform as Jamie.

'What's your name?' said the guard.

Jamie thought fast. He couldn't say Jamie – that was a human name. 'Harb,' he said, giving the name of a mean schoolboy genie he remembered from his time at the Academy.

The guard beckoned Jamie inside. 'I'm Isra Ganim, but you can call me Sir. Wanna tour?' he asked.

Isra locked the door behind them with a big silver key which he put back on his belt and led Jamie across a tiny courtyard. He nodded to a guard who unlocked a second door and Jamie followed Isra into a long, dark corridor, lit by flaming torches. The walls were black and slimy to the touch, and the smell of stale sweat and rotting food was overwhelming – even Jamie's bin had smelt better.

'These are the cells,' Isra said.

Jamie realised there were doors on each side of the corridor. He peered through the little barred window in one of the doors and saw a scared-looking prisoner staring back at him. The look in his eyes was desperate.

'Don't worry, they can't do anything to ya!' said Isra. 'You can't make wishes in a thundercloud. This one,' said Isra, pointing through a different barred window at a scary-looking genie with an eye patch, ''is Haji Kassab. He sold his wishes to humans. Not so clever now, are ya?' Isra laughed and moved onto the next cell. 'This one killed his brother and stole his money.'

Jamie shuddered as a genie with a set of gold teeth flashed him a crooked smile.

'Why aren't they banished?' asked Jamie. 'I thought that's what happened when you broke the Genie Code.'

'You've got a chance of rescue if you get banished to a bottle,' said Isra. 'Here there is no hope.' He gave a cackle. 'You've got to be really bad to end up here, but once you're in, you stay forever. We've got five floors of them!'

Jamie made sure he looked in all the cells carefully, to see which one held Methuzular, but couldn't see his old headmaster anywhere.

At the end of the corridor. Isra stopped at a spiralling stairwell and grinned. 'Of course, we keep the worst of the worst down there. In the dungeon,' said Isra and turned around. 'Come on! The tour's over!'

'But what about M—' Jamie stopped himself just in time. No one was supposed to know his old headmaster was there. Jamie suddenly had a hunch where Methuzular might be.

Isra was already halfway down the dank corridor when Jamie called out, 'Can I see inside the dungeon?'

'No visitors are allowed in there,' hissed Isra. 'Dakhil's orders.'

'Ah. I bet only brave genies go down there,' Jamie said innocently.

'The bravest of the brave,' Isra agreed proudly.

'No wonder you're too scared to show me,' said Jamie, leaning casually against the wall.

Isra's eyes flashed in the darkness and he marched back towards Jamie.

'I don't suppose you're even important enough to have a key,' continued Jamie.

'I *do* have a key!' said Isra, fumbling for the chain that swung from his belt hook. 'It's right here, see?' Isra thrust a big black key into Jamie's face. 'Only me and Dakhil have a key to this place and I'm not scared of nothing,' he said, snarling.

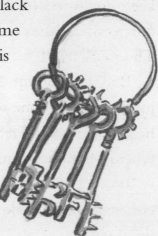

'Prove it,' said Jamie.

'I'll take you down there! But don't wee yer pantaloons if it's too spooky for you!'

Isra marched down the stairs, slid back the bolts and undid the three locks one by one.

The door creaked open and Jamie made his way carefully down the slimy steps. Isra struck a match and lit the torch that hung from the ceiling. As it spluttered into life, Jamie looked at the single cell before him. Inside, he could see a lone, dishevelled genie.

'This,' said Isra, 'is what a traitor looks like.'

CHAPTER 7

Jamie stared at Methuzular in shock. Although he already knew who this 'traitor' was, he didn't have to pretend to be surprised. It was hard to believe that the genie before him had once been the powerful, imposing headmaster of the Genie Academy. Through the bars of the tiny cell, Jamie could see that his hair was matted, his beard ragged, his face covered in dirt and his clothes tattered. He looked as if he hadn't eaten for days, and was chained to the rough wall by his ankle. There were no windows, and Jamie thought he saw something with too many legs scurry across the ground of the cell. Water dripped constantly from somewhere and a chill seeped into his very bones.

Methuzlar's eyes narrowed as he peered up at Jamie and Isra.

'I bought someone to see ya!' snarled Isra. 'Ain't I nice?'

Jamie took a step towards Methuzular and gripped the bars that separated them. By the flickering torchlight Jamie saw Methuzular suppress a gasp as he recognised Jamie.

'Not so high and mighty now, are we, Methuzular?' taunted Isra. 'Remember when you told me off for cheating in the magic carpet grand final back in the Academy? I told you I'd get my own back and it looks like I was right.'

The guard chuckled and glared at Jamie. 'And as for you! Nobody calls me scared and gets away with it! Let's see how you like being stuck in the dungeon on your own with a traitor!'

What luck! But Jamie knew he couldn't let Isra know that. He turned to plead with the genie, just as if he'd been told he was about to have a triple geography exam with a maths test sandwich. 'No! Please! Anything but that!'

Isra chuckled as he marched up the stairs. 'Stuff the Academy! I'm gonna teach you a proper lesson!' he said and the door clanged shut behind him.

When Jamie was sure that he and Methuzular were alone, he ran back to the cell bars.

The headmaster strained to smile, and reached out a hand. 'Jamie Najar,' he croaked. He sounded as if he hadn't spoken in an age. 'Where have you come from?'

'Balthazar fetched me,' explained Jamie. 'He told me everything that's happened.'

'Bad times have come to Lampville, Jamie. Dakhil never forgave me for letting you stay in the Academy. I knew he would take his revenge somehow.'

'But you must have some idea how to put things right again,' said Jamie.

Methuzular stared at the ground and shook his
head sadly. 'I've had plenty of time to think about
it,' he said sadly. 'I've turned over the possibilities
in my head a thousand times, but there's nothing I
can do.'

'I can help,' said Jamie. 'They think I'm a guard
now. I could sneak something in for you to help
you escape.'

'No magic works in a thundercloud,'

Methuzular reminded him. 'Even the Book of Wishes would be useless to me here.'

'There must be something I can do,' Jamie said. He couldn't believe he'd managed to find Methuzular just to be told it was all hopeless!

Methuzular lifted his head and studied Jamie for a moment. 'There is only one thing that might work,' he said. 'But it is very risky.'

Jamie clutched the bars. 'It's risky for me just being here, yet here I am.'

Methuzular gave Jamie a weak smile. 'I'd forgotten how determined you are, Jamie Najar,' he said. 'All right, I'll tell you. There is such a thing as a truth wish. Should a genie get close enough to Dakhil to make it, Dakhil could be forced to admit all the lies he has told.'

'Tell it to me, Methuzular,' said Jamie. 'I'll do it.'

Methuzular shook his head. 'Only the most powerful genies would even stand a chance of granting such a strong wish. To grant it means pitting genie

magic against genie magic;
Dakhil would kill anyone weaker
than him who tried and failed. I
might stand a chance, but would
never be able to get close
enough to him. There is only
one person I know who might
be powerful enough,' said

Methuzular. '*If* she can be persuaded to help. To see
her grant wishes was to watch a master at work.
She and I would try to out-do each other with our
magic and every time she was better than me.'

Methuzular's eyes grew misty and his voice
wistful as he remembered. 'I'll never forget the day
I challenged her to a transformation wish contest.
We transformed ourselves into the fastest animals
we could think of and raced around Lampville. I
magicked myself into an eagle and she became a
leopard. While I soared high in the skies, she
menaced everyone in town! Everyone was so
scared of her that they dived out of her way,
leaving the streets clear for her to win hands
down.' He laughed at the memory.

'Who was she?' asked Jamie. 'I'm sure she'll want to help.'

Methuzular sighed and leant back into the flickering shadows of his prison cell. 'Her name was Ameerah,' said Methuzular. 'She was my sister. She fell in love with a young man from your world and wished herself human so that she might marry him. It's the only wish a genie can make that is permanent. So you see, Ameerah is no longer a genie but a human. However, there is a wish in the Book of Wishes – also a very powerful wish – that can reverse it and make her a genie again, but only if she wants to be.'

'She's your sister,' said Jamie. 'Why wouldn't she want to help you?'

'When she announced that she was going to be a human, the genie world shunned her.' Methuzular looked at Jamie with shame in his eyes. 'Even I turned my back. No genie had done it before and no genie has done it since. We felt she was betraying us. I regret it now, but one thing a genie can't do is turn back time. I would understand if she wanted nothing more to do with our world.'

'Well, I've got to try,' said Jamie. 'Where will I find her?'

'You already know where to find her,' said Methuzular softly. 'Her genie blood flows in your veins.'

'Gran?' said Jamie suddenly, in a flash of inspiration. 'Granny Amy?'

Methuzular had told Jamie at the end of his last visit that he had a genie ancestor and

after all, it had been Gran who had given him the teapot that contained Balthazar – and he had noticed her pointy ears. He hadn't had a chance to talk to Gran about it since he'd been back – somehow she'd always avoided him. He'd certainly never imagined that she might be a very powerful genie – and that Methuzular was her brother!

'I didn't know immediately that you were Ameerah's grandson,' said Methuzular. 'I used the Portal of Dreams to watch over her from time to time, and when you arrived at the Academy, thought you looked familiar somehow. It wasn't until I used the portal to see where you lived and I saw her again that it all clicked into place. I am hoping that the fact that she showed you a little of the genie world means that she hasn't turned her back on us completely.'

'She'll come back,' said Jamie. 'I know she will.'

Jamie's mind was swimming with questions, but Methuzular interrupted his thoughts.

'Jamie, we don't have much time. I'm going to tell you the truth wish. It's such an important wish I learnt it off by heart,' explained Methuzular. 'Listen carefully and try to remember it.

*'May this genie now be honest
and true,
May his lies disappear
like morning dew.
May he speak free from
deceit and fuss
And may he tell only the truth to us.'*

Jamie did his best to fix it in his memory, but heard the door at the top of the stairs being unlocked.

'You filthy traitor!' Jamie bellowed, thinking quickly. 'How could you bring humans to Lampville! You deserve to rot forever!'

'That's the way,' said Isra, standing at the top of the stairs. 'We'll make a guard out of you yet. Now come on, you've had your fun! There's work to be done!'

'Coming, Sir!' called Jamie.

'Blow out the lantern!'

instructed Isra. 'Leave the rat to the darkness he deserves.'

Jamie felt terrible, but had to keep his cover. His eyes met Methuzular's, and saw hope in them once more. Then he blew out the light.

It was only as he followed Isra down the corridor and out through the courtyard to the prison office that Jamie understood the magnitude of what he had to do. He had to persuade his gran to come back to Lampville and agree to become a genie again. Then they would have to find the Book of Wishes and the wish to make that happen. *Then* his gran would have to try to defeat Dakhil with the truth wish. But the very first thing he had to do was get away from the prison.

CHAPTER 8

Isra took him to the prison office and settled into a chair, scratched his belly and yawned. Jamie's mind was still swirling. He had already guessed that his gran was a genie – but it seemed very strange to actually *know* that she was. Or had been, at least. She'd always had a twinkle in her eye but Jamie couldn't imagine her granting wishes and zooming about on a flying carpet. Now it turned out that not only had she been a genie, but she'd been an extremely powerful one too!

'Get me some water, boy,' said Isra, interrupting his thoughts.

'Yes, Sir,' said Jamie, heading over to a low table littered with grubby mugs. As Jamie poured water from a grimy flask, a strange machine on the guard's desk began to rumble like thunder. Jamie jumped in surprise.

'What's the matter?' said Isra. 'Never seen a cloudphone before?'

The cloudphone looked a bit like Jamie's dad's laptop, and it glowed as it rumbled. The screen was a mass of swirling clouds, but as Isra turned a dial on the side, the clouds swirled into the shape of a face. It was like looking at a ghost.

As soon as Jamie glimpsed the face he knew he was in trouble. He gave Isra his drink and backed away out of sight.

 'Lampville Jail! This is Dakhil Ganim!' barked the cloudphone.

His voice sounded like it was coming from a very long way away but he spoke with the unmistakable authority Jamie had heard many times before. When Isra heard Dakhil's voice, he jumped out of his chair, spilling his drink, and gave the cloudphone a little salute.

'Good morning, Sir!' he said.

Jamie held his breath. He didn't want Dakhil to know anyone else was in the room and he didn't want Isra to have a reason to mention him.

'I'll be coming for an inspection tomorrow,' barked Dakhil. 'We need to make sure our special guest isn't causing any trouble.'

'Your special guest is still safely chained to the wall,' chuckled Isra.

'That's all very well,' said Dakhil, 'but I want to see for myself.'

Isra nodded and saluted again. 'Very well, Sir, we shall be waiting for you.'

Jamie breathed a sigh of relief as Dakhil finished the conversation. 'Well, till tomorrow, then.'

'One other thing, Sir,' said Isra, glancing in Jamie's direction. Jamie's heart began to hammer. 'The trainee is working out very well indeed.'

Dakhil paused and peered into the cloudphone. 'What trainee?' he asked.

'The one you sent from the Academy,' said Isra. 'He was even brave enough to go down into the dungeon!'

'What?!' bellowed Dakhil. 'You let someone see Methuzular?'

'Only the trainee, Sir,' said Isra. 'As you sent him, I thought it would be fine.'

'I didn't send anyone!' yelled Dakhil.

'B–b–but he's right here,' stammered Isra, obviously confused.

Isra began to quiver and reached out a hand for Jamie. Jamie dodged away, raced out of the office and made for the main door.

'Isra!' Jamie heard the voice bellow from the cloudphone. 'What have you done?'

'Emergency!' Jamie shouted at the guard as he reached the main door. 'Open the door!'

The guard nodded, then unlocked and opened the door.

Suddenly Isra appeared. 'Emergency! Close the door!' he yelled. 'Close the door!'

Two sets of orders was too much for him, and now he didn't know what to do. As the guard hestitated, Jamie darted through the narrow gap just as the door clanged shut.

'Open the door! *Open* the door!' Isra shouted as Jamie sped away, disappearing into the bustle of Lampville.

'Make your mind up!' tutted the confused guard.

By the time Isra got out, Jamie was nowhere to be seen.

CHAPTER 9

Jamie ran back to Ivana's shop as quickly as he could.

'I've got to get back to the Academy,' Jamie gasped. 'I've got to leave – now. Someone probably saw me come here. It's not safe to stay.'

'You'll be needing these,' said Fadiyah, getting out a black waistcoat and pair of pantaloons.

'And don't forget this,' said Ivana, handing over a black turban. 'To cover your ears,' she explained.

As Jamie made his way to the Academy, his mind began to race. Surely the guards would be on the look-out for him, but at least Isra hadn't realised that Jamie was human. They would be searching for a genie boy rather than Jamie, so hopefully his cover wasn't completely blown.

When Jamie got to the Academy, he immediately made his way to Balthazar's shed. Jamie peered through the window and saw that his friend was fast asleep on the cloud chair. Jamie tapped the window and Balthazar jumped to attention, clattering into a bucket and getting tangled in a makeshift washing line.

'Wass that?!' he spluttered, trying to salute and getting a finger wedged up his nose. 'Wasn't sleeping, Sir! Just examining my eyelids!'

When Balthazar saw Jamie standing at the window, he breathed a sigh of relief and rushed over to let him in. 'What happened?!' he asked. 'Did you see Methuzular?'

Jamie nodded and told Balthazar everything.

When Jamie had finished, Balthazar stroked his chin thoughtfully. 'Who'd have thought it?' he said. 'Your gran a powerful genie! We need to get to the Portal of Dreams so you can go home and bring her back. It's the most reliable way for us to get to the human world..'

'While I'm gone you need to find out where Dakhil is keeping the Book of Wishes,' said Jamie as he got changed back into his human school uniform.

'Find the Book of Wishes,' Balthazar said. 'How? Dakhil isn't keeping it in his office like Methuzular used to.'

'You'll have to think of something,' said Jamie.

'But if I get caught . . .' Balthazar shuddered.

'Then don't get caught,' said Jamie. 'It worked for me!' He looked at his worried friend and gave him a reassuring pat on the back. 'It might be easier than persuading my gran to come back.'

'Of course she'll want to come back!' Balthazar said. 'It beats bingo, doesn't it?'

Jamie and Balthazar waited in the shed until it grew dark. Then Balthazar loaded his trolley with polish and dustpans and said to Jamie, 'In you get!' They had decided the best way to smuggle Jamie into the Academy was for him to hide inside the cleaning trolley and then Balthazar would wheel him to the room where the Portal of Dreams was kept. As a cleaner, Balthazar had a special key that let him in to all the rooms in the Academy.

Balthazar had made a little den

for Jamie between the two shelves of the trolley.
'I'll disguise you,' he explained as he draped a
yellow duster over Jamie's head. 'And together
we'll make a clean getaway. *Clean* getaway, get it?'

But Jamie was too nervous to laugh. He made
a peephole for himself. By the light of a full moon
high in the sky, he could see guards patrolling
outside the Academy.

'There are more guards than usual,' whispered
Balthazar out of the corner of his mouth. 'Word

must have spread about your little adventure in the prison. We'll have to be extra careful.'

Balthazar slowly bumped the trolley towards the Academy. He was a rubbish driver and swerved left and right until Jamie was sure he was going to get travel sick.

Jamie realised that they were in the main corridor – he recognised all the portraits of important-looking genies, which hung from the walls. The corridor was deserted, but Jamie's heart jumped as he heard footsteps coming around the corner.

'Don't move a muscle!' said Balthazar, rearranging the dusters.

'Balthazar Najar!' barked a voice. Jamie's blood ran cold. It belonged to Dabir, Dakhil's son. Dabir had taunted Jamie when he'd been at the Academy, and had once trapped him in a lamp and threatened to keep him as a pet for the rest of his days. That wasn't something Jamie would forget in a hurry.

'You look nervous,' sneered Dabir. 'What are you up to?'

'Me, Sir? N-nothing, Sir,' stuttered Balthazar.

Dabir stopped the trolley with his foot. 'Then you won't mind if I have a look in your trolley,' he said. 'There was trouble down at the prison this afternoon. But you'd know nothing about that, would you?'

'Of course not,' said Balthazar.

Jamie could barely breathe. If Dabir found him, they could both end up in prison like Methuzular and no one would stop Dakhil. Jamie froze as he heard Dabir searching the shelf above him. He felt Dabir's hand brush past the pile of dusters to his left. If he moved just one of them, Jamie would be spotted instantly.

Suddenly there were more footsteps in the corridor and Dabir spun away. 'Who goes there?' he snapped. 'It's after lights out!'

'Adeel Maloof,' came the reply. 'I'm bringing sandwiches for the guards' supper.'

Jamie heard Dabir licking his lips. Dabir had always been greedy.

'Quality control!' he snapped, snatching a sandwich. 'Very good,' mumbled Dabir between chomps. 'Give me another!' He looked up angrily. 'Haven't you got work to do, Balthazar?' barked Dabir.

Jamie breathed a sigh of relief as the trolley began to move again.

'We're lucky Adeel showed up when he did,' said Balthazar.

'I don't know if luck had anything to do with it,' said Jamie. 'If I know Adeel, he was looking out for us. What was Dabir doing?'

'Patrolling the corridors,' explained Balthazar, stopping in front of a classroom. 'He's head boy now, so it's his job to make sure nobody leaves their bed at night.'

Balthazar unlocked the door, pushed the trolley inside and locked it again behind him. Only then did he let Jamie clamber out.

'The sooner we get you home the better,' he said, grabbing the shimmering cloth and unveiling the Portal of Dreams.

The portal was a screen about as tall as Balthazar, and genies used it to watch the human world and to travel accurately between the two worlds without wishes. It was like a huge interactive television set.

Jamie stood in front of the screen, remembering that it was controlled like a high-tec video game. The right hand controlled left and right and up and down while the left controlled forward and back. He began to move his arms like a slow-motion kung-fu fighter, and soon the Earth appeared through the swirling clouds. He guided the image on the screen until he was looking at his hometown and pushed towards his school. He realised that he'd better return there and come up with an excuse about why he needed to go home – otherwise Miss Rothwell would miss him, and who knew what she'd do? She might get the police on the case!

Through the portal he could see that the spelling test was still going on.

'Spell *establish*,' Miss Rothwell instructed.

'You humans have it sooo easy!' snorted Balthazar. 'That's not hard, is it?'

'Well, how do you spell it, clever clogs?' asked Jamie.

Balthazar scratched his chin. 'Erm . . . *S, T* . . .' He hesitated. 'Is there a letter *shh*?'

Jamie shook his head and guided the portal down the school corridor and into the boys' toilets. 'I'll be back with my gran as soon as possible,' said Jamie.

Jamie put his left leg through the portal's screen. It shimmered like a soap bubble and for a brief moment he had one foot in the Academy

and another in a toilet cubicle. Jamie's tummy tickled as he stepped into the cubicle.

Balthazar waved at him. 'Good luck,' he said. 'I'll leave the portal right here. No one is using it now regular classes are cancelled so you can use it to come back as soon as possible.'

At that very moment there was a *rat-a-tat-tat* on the cubicle door. 'Are you in there, Jamie?' called Dylan. 'Miss Rothwell sent me to find you. You've been gone fifteen minutes. You've missed the spelling test.'

Despite everything, Jamie couldn't help but feel proud of his timing.

He came out of the cubicle and smiled at his worried friend. 'I've just been back to the Academy,' he explained. 'There's terrible trouble up there and only my gran can help.'

Dylan shook his head. He'd been wrong about his friend – it was clear Jamie wasn't really as mad as a gerbil on a trampoline, he was as mad as a walrus on a bouncy castle! 'You need to come back to class,' said Dylan. 'You've got some explaining to do!'

CHAPTER 10

Jamie followed Dylan into the corridor, but he knew he couldn't go back to lessons.

'I've got to go home,' said Jamie, pushing open the outside door. 'You'll have to make some excuse for me – sorry!'

'But Miss Rothwell will be furious!' said Dylan. 'What's she going to say if I tell her you've gone to rescue some genies?!'

'Tell her my mum came to pick me up because

I had a headache,' said Jamie as he headed into the playground.

Jamie made it home in record time. He found the spare key that was hidden in the back garden and let himself in. Dad would be at work and Mum would be collecting his baby brother Paulie from playgroup – he and his gran would be able to talk in private.

'Gran!' he called.

'In here,' came the reply from the front room. Jamie could hear the TV blaring. He pushed open the door and found Gran lying on the floor with her leg behind her shoulder. She was wearing a bright pink leotard, a pair of blue tracksuit bottoms and a blue and pink striped headband to keep her curls of grey hair out of her eyes.

'You've caught me in the middle of my yoga,' she explained. 'What are you doing home, anyway? Have they expelled you for being too brainy?'

Jamie watched Gran re-arrange herself into a very uncomfortable-looking position, mirroring the man on the television. This time, both her feet

were touching her ears. Jamie winced. He marched over to the TV and switched it off. 'I know all about genies,' said Jamie. 'You've got a lot to tell me, Gran. Or should I say, Ameerah?'

'That's a name I haven't heard in a long time,' whispered Gran, suddenly looking serious. Or as serious as she could do with her feet behind her ears.

Jamie crouched beside her as she untangled herself and took her hands in his. 'I know who you used to be,' he said. 'And how you fell in love and wished yourself human. I also know that you wanted me to find out about it too, sooner or later. That's why you gave me the teapot, isn't it?'

Gran nodded her head. 'I thought you should know a bit about where your old grandma came from, and I thought the wishes might be fun for you, too.'

Jamie quickly filled his gran in on what had happened a few days ago — how he had spent a term at the Genie Academy. He wanted to ask her lots of questions, but he knew he didn't have time.

'You have to come back,' he said, cutting to the chase. 'There's trouble in Lampville and they need your help.'

'I'm very happy with my human life now, Jamie, thank you. I don't need to go back to wishing.'

'But you can't want the genie world to be doomed!'

'It was hard to leave my friends and family . . . I've missed them dearly. But they just couldn't understand why I fell in love with a human. The things they said before I left! Then they never spoke to me again. I doubt they even care if I'm alive.' There was bitterness in Gran's voice that Jamie had never heard before.

'It's not true!' Jamie told her. 'Methuzular said he watches over you in the Portal of Dreams and he regrets ever being so mean to you about Granddad.'

At the mention of Methuzular, Gran's interest rose a little. 'My brother? When did he tell you that?'

Jamie hesitated. He didn't want to upset Gran by telling her about the terrible state Methuzular was in. But he had to. However, as he described everything to her, she didn't grow sad – she got mad!

'Dakhil was always mean,' Gran said, her eyes blazing with anger. 'Methuzular and I tried to stand up for him when he was teased at school, but he never wanted our friendship, never wanted anybody's help. He always made the nastiest wishes. Once he wished my hair into snakes and my ears were nipped to pieces! Another time he flooded the whole of the girls' dormitory with frogs. We stayed on the top bunks all night long and didn't get a wink of sleep!'

'That's why you have to come back,' said Jamie, pulling Gran to her feet. 'You're the only person powerful enough to stop him.'

Gran suddenly tore off her headband with a flick of her wrist. 'You're right, Jamie,' she said, heading for the door. 'And brothers and sisters should stick together, no matter what! Come on, dawdle drawers! Those evil genies won't defeat themselves.'

Jamie smiled and chased after her. Somehow things didn't seem so bad with Gran around.

As they got to the front gate, they saw Mum and baby Paulie. 'Why aren't you at school?' she called as she dropped a bag of nappies on the ground.

'It's Bring Your Gran to School day,' Gran called as they marched briskly down the road.

'But surely you're not allowed out of school during the day —' Mum started to say as Jamie hurried after Gran.

'Exactly,' agreed Gran. 'Which is why we have to get back right now!'

Jamie and Gran sneaked through the playground and into the school. Time was flying by – they had to get to the Portal of Dreams and return to Lampville as quickly as possible. When they crept into the toilets they found Dylan washing his hands. He jumped when he saw them.

'I told Miss Rothwell you'd gone home. What's your gran doing here?!' he gasped.

'I was once a powerful genie, don't you know!' trilled Gran.

'She's coming with me back to the genie world. We've got some things to put right,' said Jamie matter of factly. 'We need to use the magic Portal of Dreams hidden in the toilet cubicle.'

Dylan looked at him in disbelief. 'Your whole family is as barking as an open day at a kennel,' he said.

Just then, the door to one of the cubicles flew open and Balthazar Najar burst out. He was hot and flustered and his forehead was covered in sweat.

Dylan took a step back. 'W-who are you?' he stammered.

'This is Balthazar Najar,' announced Jamie. 'He was the genie that used to live in my teapot.'

Dylan rubbed his eyes and slowly shook his head.

Balthazar grabbed Jamie's arm. 'You've been gone too long!' he said. 'Things are getting worse. They hunted for the genie that sneaked into the jail but found nothing. Dakhil has tightened security at the prison and then, last night, I heard him talking to Isra on his cloudphone. He talked about getting rid of Methuzular permanently.'

Jamie felt a shiver run down his spine.

'He's plotting something big, Jamie,' continued Balthazar. 'The trainee genies are spending all their time practising marching and fighting. We need Ameerah. Did she say she'd help?'

'Yes,' said Gran. 'I'll come with you.'

Balthazar turned to see Jamie's gran. He gave a little bow. 'Ameerah,' he said. 'It is an honour.' He held his hand out to her and helped her through the Portal of Dreams before following her himself.

'Who's Ameerah? Who's marching and fighting? What's going on?!' wailed Dylan.

'I'll explain everything when I get back,' promised Jamie, 'but right now we're in a rush.'

And with that, he stepped through the Portal of Dreams, leaving an open-mouthed Dylan behind, staring in amazement at an empty toilet cubicle.

CHAPTER 11

The portal rippled like the surface of a pond as they made their way back through the shimmering screen. Sunshine streamed through the stained-glass window at the far end of the classroom.

Gran looked around the room and grinned. 'Still smells of dusty waistcoats,' she said to Jamie. 'Some things never change!'

'We have to be quick,' said Balthazar. 'Here are

your genie clothes,' he said to Jamie. 'And I've got you some, too, Ameerah.' He handed her a set of black pantaloons and waistcoat.

'Who wears black?' said Gran. 'I'm a Najar, red or dead! Where's my red waistcoat?'

'Nowadays everyone wears black,' explained Jamie.

Once they had got changed, they crept outside to see all the trainee genies marching in long straight lines.

Jamie's gran wrinkled her nose in dismay. 'Genies shouldn't march in time,' she said, 'they should live lightly and shine brightly.'

'Not when Dakhil's in charge,' said Balthazar. 'It's like he's turning the trainee genies into his own personal army.'

It was true. The rows of black-clad genies looked a lot like soldiers. Jamie saw Adeel at the front of one of the lines. As he was watching, Adeel glanced up and caught Jamie's eye.

Balthazar led Jamie and Gran down the far side of the Academy wall. Suddenly Balthazar froze and held a finger to his lips for quiet, and then slowly pointed. There were guards just ahead. Balthazar shoved Jamie and his gran into the cover of a cloud bush. One guard heard the rustle of leaves and looked round.

'Who goes there?' he shouted. 'This area is out of bounds!'

'Only me!' said Balthazar, taking a cloth from his pocket and waving it like a little white flag at the guard. 'I'm cleaning the windows.'

'Nobody's allowed to use this path,' sniffed the guard, brandishing his sword towards Balthazar's throat. 'Dakhil's orders.'

'I'm s–s–s–sorry,' Balthazar stammered. 'It was him that told me to make the windows sparkle!'

The guard looked at Balthazar and then aimed a huge spitball at the window. 'You've missed a bit,' he said with a sneer on his face. 'Finish this up and don't come round here again!'

'Of course, Sir,' said Balthazar. 'I'll get right on with it.' He gave a little salute as the guard left.

'Spitballs! Disgusting,' growled Gran. 'If I see him again I'll give him a piece of my mind.'

'I don't think that's a very good idea,' said Balthazar, winking at Jamie. 'You need every piece you've got left! Come on. We have to hurry. This is Dakhil's private path. If the guard finds out I was lying he'll turn us into giant spitballs!'

Balthazar led Jamie and Gran into a clump of cloud trees. When they were safely out of sight, he explained where they were going. 'I searched all over the school for the Book of Wishes but it wasn't anywhere. Then I started to wonder why this path is always so heavily guarded. Only Dakhil is allowed to use it, but it only leads to these boring old trees. So one evening, after I'd finished all of my jobs, I decided to follow Dakhil to find out why he came here. I had to be careful not to be seen, and by the time I got to the trees he had already disappeared. I was about to head back to the Academy when I noticed this.' Balthazar pointed to the ground. A faint trail of footprints weaved its way away from the trees. 'Look where they lead.' Balthazar parted the branches of a low-hanging tree and pointed to a dark shape on the horizon. 'Alim Tower. I reckon that's where Dakhil is keeping the Book of Wishes.'

A shiver ran down Jamie's spine. Alim Tower had been deserted for many years. Some of its turrets had fallen to the ground and the tower was said to be haunted. When Dabir had imprisoned Jamie in a lamp, he had locked him in the tower. He never wanted to set foot in there again.

'Let's go,' said Balthazar. 'We've no time to lose.'

They made their way across a cloud field, careful not to be seen. At the foot of the tower was a huge, imposing door, which Balthazar pushed open. 'Dakhil's very careless about locking it. He knows that other genies are too scared to set foot inside.'

The door opened onto a spiral staircase, which led to a room halfway up the tower – the very one in which Dabir had hidden Jamie when he trapped him inside a lamp. When Jamie was last there, it had been a dusty old storeroom filled with broken furniture and old statues, but now Dakhil had transformed it with plush rugs and a heavy desk into his own private office.

'I'm sure the Book of Wishes is here somewhere,' said Balthazar. 'There's no other place it can be. We just have to find it.'

They spread out to search. Jamie opened a battered old trunk that was lying under the window and rummaged through it, but there was no Book of Wishes. Then he looked in a cupboard in the far corner of the room. He pushed all the waistcoats and cloaks to one side and found some dusty old portraits. He pulled them out of the way, but there was no Book of Wishes hidden behind them.

Balthazar shook his head. 'We've looked everywhere.'

'Maybe we've missed the most obvious place,' said Jamie, as his eyes came to rest on the bookshelf.

'I've checked every single book,' said Balthazar. 'Not one of them is the Book of Wishes. Besides, hiding a book in a bookshelf isn't very sneaky, is it?'

'You should never judge a book by its cover,' said Gran. 'And if you're as sneaky as Dakhil, you might swap things around a bit.'

Jamie had seen the Book of Wishes before, and tried to remember what it looked like. He searched along the shelf and took out a big, heavy book that looked the same size. On the cover was *How to Polish Your Lamp – the Genie Way!*

'That book has a lot of pages for such a simple subject,' said Jamie.

'And look,' said Gran, pointing at the pages. 'The cover is brand new but the pages inside are all yellow.'

Jamie flipped open the book to reveal the Book of Wishes hidden inside.

'You are geniuses, both of you!' gasped Balthazar, giving them a high five.

Gran leafed through the book. Each of the ancient pages were covered in golden writing that seemed to shimmer in the light. 'Every wish that ever was,' she said quietly. 'It's beautiful.'

There were wishes to bring lamp posts to life, wishes to turn people into every animal from an aardvark to a zebra and wishes that could turn your nose into a volcano.

'Look!' Balthazar cried. 'A wish that can turn your feet into springs! Can we look at that one pleeeeasc!' Balthazar began to boing around the room with excitement and knocked over a plant pot, spilling soil onto the floor. 'Oops,' he said, bending down to tidy it up.

'Quick,' said Jamie. 'We need to find the *turn me back into a genie* wish. Let's get out of here now and take the Book of Wishes with us!'

Just then Jamie heard something. He strained his ears and listened again. He couldn't be sure, but he thought he'd heard the creak of the heavy downstairs door. Jamie tiptoed towards the office door and listened. He could hear footsteps, he was sure of it.

'There's someone coming!' he hissed. 'Hide!'

Gran flipped the book closed and put it back on the shelf. The footsteps were getting closer and closer. They all scanned the room for a hiding place. Jamie's eyes came to rest on the cupboard. 'In here!' he said, scurrying to the cupboard door. 'Cupboards seem to be my favourite place to hide in Lampville!' They all hid as best they could behind the dusty old cloaks.

The door was flung open. 'Good marching practice!' said a voice, which Jamie immediately recognised as Dakhil's. 'The genie army is nearly ready. We'll get rid of Methuzular, convince the Genie Congress to let us have our way, and then we can wreak our revenge on the human world for what they made my father do! Our army will have the humans doing *our* bidding for a change.'

'I can't wait, Dad,' chuckled Dabir, clapping his hands in delight.

Jamie heard the creak of Dakhil's chair as the nasty genie sat down. They'd just have to stay put until they left.

'Hang this in the cupboard for me!' ordered Dakhil suddenly.

Jamie, Gran and Balthazar all held their breath as the cupboard door opened and Jamie watched through a gap as Dabir absent-mindedly hung his father's waistcoat on a hook and then closed the door behind him.

Jamie could feel the other two relaxing beside him.

But just then Dakhil called out, 'What's this? There's dirt on the floor! Someone's been here!'

Jamie turned to Balthazar, his eyes blazing. 'I thought you'd tidied the plant up!' he hissed.

'I started to,' said Balthazar, his bottom lip beginning to tremble, 'but then you got all distracted so I kind of forgot to finish.'

'Well, don't just stand there Dabir!' barked Dakhil. 'Search the place!'

It seemed like ages before they got to the cupboard, but they eventually did. The door flung open again and Dakhil clasped his hands together and spoke a wish.

'*Stars of gold and stars of light,*

Help me make this darkness bright!'

Any hopes they had of not being found disappeared as Dakhil breathed out and an orb of light appeared in his hands. Dakhil released the sphere and it floated into the air, coming to rest on the ceiling of the cupboard.

'Jamie and Balthazar!' Dabir gasped as he saw them.

But to their surprise, Dakhil began to laugh. 'Perfect!' he cackled. 'There were rumours that there was a human boy in Lampville, but I thought it was just a silly young genie and his even dottier mother telling stories. Turns out it was true after all!'

Dakhil reached in, grabbed Jamie by the ear and dragged him into his office. Gran and Balthazar followed them out. 'And a wrinkly old human accomplice too!' Dakhil gave Jamie and his gran a cruel smirk. 'No doubt trying to steal my Book of Wishes. Finally I have the excuse I need to banish the traitor Balthazar Najar for good. Guards! Seize them!' he shouted and Jamie's heart sank as three guards, who had obviously been standing outside the door, grabbed hold of them.

There would be no stopping Dakhil now.

CHAPTER 12

Dakhil settled into his chair and looked Jamie, Gran and Balthazar up and down.

'Now things are starting to make sense,' said Dakhil looking at Jamie. '*You* broke into Lampville Jail, didn't you?'

Jamie nodded his head.

Dakhil clapped his hands in triumph. 'I'm *so* glad you came back, Jamie Najar. You've made my plan *much* easier to achieve! When I parade you in

front of the Genie Congress and tell them
I found you trying to steal the Book of
Wishes from my office, they'll see it as
an act of war – and they'll let me do
anything to stop you.'

Dakhil turned to Gran. 'You are
the one piece of this puzzle I can't
figure out. Jamie might need an old bag to carry
away the Book of Wishes, but wouldn't he prefer
one with handles?' He laughed at his own joke.

Gran looked at Dakhil for the first time, her
eyes filled with venom. 'We have met before,
Dakhil Ganim!' she said. 'You may not remember
me, but I remember you. You once turned my
beautiful blond curls into snarling snakes and
when I left the genie world, your taunts were the
cruellest of them all!'

Dakhil stared into Gran's blazing eyes for a
moment and then gasped when he recognised her.
'Ameerah?' he asked.

Gran nodded her head and Dakhil
began to chuckle. The chuckle grew
into a deep booming laugh and he

thumped the table in delight. 'This gets better and better! The traitor sister of a traitor headmaster! I can see now how I can make it look. Methuzular brought Jamie to the Academy as a human spy, and sent his sister to live with humans to get them ready to fight the genies. The three of you were working with Balthazar to infiltrate the genie world, steal the Book of Wishes and give humans domination over genies! But I, Dakhil Ganim, have foiled your plot! Before long I'll be leading my army through the Portal of Dreams and into the human world where I intend to make them serve us. My revenge will taste very sweet indeed.'

'You can't!' said Balthazar.

'Oh, but I can,' replied Dakhil. 'And as for you,' Dakhil shook his head in mock dismay, 'secretly helping the humans all this time . . . I believe that counts as using your wishes for evil. That's rule two of the Genie Code broken. You were on your final warning, so I think we all know where you're going!'

Dakhil inhaled deeply and blew out a sparkling wish. A small glass bottle appeared on the desk.

Balthazar's eyes grew
wide with fear. Dakhil
flashed his teeth like a
shark.

'Wait!' said Gran.
'Only the Congress can
banish him to a bottle.'

Dakhil raised an
eyebrow. 'Thanks to you
and your grandson's
meddling, Ameerah Najar, the Genie Congress
will let me do whatever I want!'

Dabir handed his father the Book of Wishes
from the bookshelf, and Dakhil turned to the
appropriate page. 'You are a disgrace to genies,' he
said to Balthazar, 'and, as leader of the Genie
Congress, it gives me great pleasure to banish you
to a bottle at the bottom of the sea!'

Dabir clapped in delight as his father inhaled
once more, closed his eyes and blew a wish
towards Balthazar.

'No!' yelled Jamie, but a guard grabbed him and
he could only watch helplessly as the wish

enveloped Balthazar and shrunk him to the size of a flea. Jamie heard Balthazar's tiny scream as he was whisked on a cloud of stars towards the neck of the bottle and flung inside.

'Can I do the banishing, Dad?' begged Dabir. 'Pleeeease!'

Dakhil smiled and nodded. Dabir giggled, closed the bottle with a cork, clapped his hands and the bottle disappeared.

'The apple doesn't fall far from the tree I see,' muttered Gran.

'That's how we deal with traitors here,' announced Dakhil, dusting his hands. 'I have caught two human spies, banished a traitor and set up my invasion of the human world. Not bad for a day's work!'

'Genies are *supposed* to help humans,' said Gran. 'It's what we do.'

Dakhil turned his attention towards the old lady. 'Who are you to tell me about genies?' he scoffed, looking Gran up and down. 'You lost that right the day you chose the human world over the genie world! Take them to the top of the tower and lock them up,' said Dakhil to the guards. 'No one will find you there – apart from the ghosts. I still need time to train my army for the attack. When I am ready, I will come and fetch you and use you as proof that all I have told the Genie Congress is true. Then I will reunite you with Methuzular in Lampville Jail where you can live out the rest of your days as one big, happy family.'

The guards grabbed Jamie and Gran and marched them up to a small, dirty room with a tiny barred window at the very top of the tower. Dabir unlocked the door and the guards threw them inside. 'Don't even think about wishing yourself free – this room is lined with thunderclouds.' The last thing they saw as the door closed was Dabir's sneering face.

Jamie leapt to his feet and tugged at the door handle. It was no surprise to find it was locked. He tried pulling on the window bars but they didn't budge either.

Jamie slumped down next to his gran and punched the floor in frustration. 'It's hopeless,' he said.

Gran gave him a reassuring squeeze. 'It's never hopeless, Jamie,' she said. 'You've done a lot that you once thought impossible. We need the Book of Wishes to turn me back into a genie, but we also need the truth wish you said Methuzular taught to you. Can you remember it?'

Jamie shook his head. What use was the truth wish now? With Balthazar banished and the two of them locked in a tower room they'd never get the chance to use it anyway.

Gran saw what Jamie was thinking and gave him a warm smile. 'We must be ready to take any chance we get,' she said.

Jamie racked his brains and tried to remember the words that Methuzular had spoken. Although it was only earlier that morning, so much had happened that his mind was filled with worry rather than wishes.

'I . . . I can't remember it,' he said.

Gran stroked her chin. 'Since coming back to Lampville, I've started to remember all sorts of things I thought I'd long forgotten. The truth wish is in there somewhere,' she said, tapping her forehead. 'It has to be! I used it all the time when I was young to get Methuzular into trouble with Mum and Dad.'

Gran laughed, but Jamie couldn't imagine the mighty Methuzular being told off by anyone!

'The wish'll be somewhere in your head too,' she continued. 'We just need to close our eyes, concentrate and try to remember it together.'

Jamie thought back to the jail. As he concentrated he heard Methuzular's voice echo in his ears.

'*May this genie now be honest and true,*' he said.

Gran's eyes popped open. 'What was that?' she asked.

'*May this genie now be honest and true!*' said Jamie, more confidently this time.

'That's ringing a bell!' she said. *'May this genie now be honest and true. May . . . may his mouth turn yellow and his eyelids blue?* No that's not right!'

Jamie laughed and while his guard was down the next line came to him in a flash.

'May his lies disappear like morning dew!' he spluttered.

Gran and Jamie high-fived and they closed their eyes to concentrate some more. Suddenly they opened their eyes at the same time.

'Got it!' they said together.

'May he speak free from deceit and fuss!' said Jamie.

'And may he tell only the truth to us,' sang Gran.

Gran and Jamie gave each other a triumphant hug and danced around the room laughing. But as their laughter died away Jamie's heart sank. Remembering the wish was only half the battle. How would they ever get the chance to use it?

CHAPTER 13

The following morning, Dabir arrived with a plate of food and passed it under the door.

'I hope you like stale cloud bread,' he said. 'It's all you're getting from now on. And this door will never be opened – so there's no chance of overpowering a guard!'

After their disgusting breakfast, Gran practised the truth wish some more. It had been a long time since she'd had to grant a wish and she needed time to find the special place in her head where magic could happen. By lunchtime they were both ready for a break.

'Did you miss magic when you became human, Gran?' asked Jamie.

Gran gazed through the barred window wistfully and smiled. 'When I was changing your mum's dirty nappies or de-slugging the garden it would have been handy,' she said. 'But what I lost when I gave up being a genie was more than made up for by the love of your granddad. Do you remember him?'

Jamie shook his head. 'Not really,' he admitted sadly.

'He was a wonderful man,' she said. 'Handsome and clever and kind and gentle.'

Jamie smiled. One of the things he did remember was his grandfather magicking ten pence pieces from his ear at Christmas.

'I first saw him when I was eighteen through the Portal of Dreams. He was the same age as me and was working for a very unpleasant farmer. The farmer said if he didn't cut the crop by sundown he wouldn't get paid. He wished for the strength of twenty men and I crept through the portal to help. Your grandfather couldn't believe his luck!' giggled Gran. 'He cleared that field in no time. I was going back to Lampville when out of the corner of his eye he saw me hidden behind a hay bale. I was about to flee when he caught me by the arm.'

'What did you do?' gasped Jamie.

'I struggled free and he watched me disappear through the portal. He didn't know whether I was a fairy or an angel or something else entirely. Over the next few years I watched him whenever I could, and did my best to grant his wishes. He would always say to people, "I am the luckiest man alive; a guardian angel watches over me!" As time went on, I fell in love with him until I could bear it no longer; I wanted to become human so that I could be close to him every day. But when I told Methuzular my plans he grew angry, and my parents were even worse. In a way, I can understand it – to them I was turning my back on their love for the love of someone I hardly knew.

I had to ask the Genie Congress for permission to live on Earth and reluctantly they gave it to me, on the condition that I would have to give up being a genie completely. So I wished myself human and said goodbye to the genie world forever – or so I thought.'

'Did Granddad recognise you?' asked Jamie.

'Instantly,' said Gran, smiling. 'He said, "I always knew you'd come back and now that you have, I really am the luckiest man alive." I told him all about who I had been, and amazingly he believed me! His parents never knew about my genie past, nor did your mother – they always thought I was an orphan, which in a way I was. For many years we lived the happiest life we could and I stopped thinking about the world I'd left behind.'

Jamie smiled. It was such a lovely story that for a moment he had managed to forget they were prisoners of Dakhil in a gloomy faraway tower. Then a thought came to him. 'If you'd decided to leave the genie world behind,' he said, 'why did you give me that teapot for my birthday?'

A twinkle appeared in Gran's eye and she ruffled his hair. 'I often thought about Lampville, especially when your grandfather died. Then, one Sunday morning, I was at a car boot sale when I spotted the teapot. I knew it was a genie teapot instantly, of course. My first thought was to release the genie myself — if one was trapped inside — but then I thought I'd give you the chance to find out a little about genies. Of course I didn't expect you to find out about your heritage quite so soon or that it would bring you here.' Gran cast her gaze around the desolate tower room. She pulled herself to her feet and helped Jamie up too. 'Breaktime's over,' she said with a smile. 'Now we have some more practising to do. I need you to help me find that special place in my mind. There's a part of me that will always be a tiny bit genie, but you were at the Academy more recently than me!'

The minutes and hours in the tower began to blur. They spent their time practising the truth wish and sharing stories. As they talked, they could occasionally hear the raised voices of Dabir and

Dakhil outside shouting instructions to the young genies marching in the grounds of the Academy. The training had been stepped up in preparation for the attack.

Many times their thoughts turned to escape, but the bars were wedged tightly in the window and even if they managed to prise them loose, they were far too high up to jump. Jamie had considered yelling to the genies while they marched up and down, but Gran pointed out that they couldn't be sure who they could trust. If word reached Dakhil that they had been causing trouble, he would only make things worse for them.

That night, Jamie was woken by a tap on the window bars. At first he thought he must be hearing things and settled back down to sleep. The tap came again and this time Jamie got up to see what it was.

There was Adeel Maloof grinning at him in the moonlight. 'Surprise!' he said. 'I brought a couple of old friends to see you.'

Jamie peered through the bars and saw that

Adeel was riding his magic carpet, Sunray. Behind him floated Threadbare, the carpet Jamie had learnt to fly in his term at the Academy.

'I . . . I . . . I don't believe it!' said Jamie. 'How did you know where to find us?'

'Dabir,' said Adeel with a shake of his head. 'He's such a boaster. After I saw you across the parade ground, I went to find you at Balthazar's shed. I returned whenever I could but you were never there, and I didn't see Balthazar cleaning either. I knew Dakhil had to have you imprisoned somewhere. I thought you might be at Lampville Jail, but Dabir started boasting about his prisoners in the tower. I put two and two together and knew it must have been you.'

'Well, you're almost right,' said Jamie. 'Balthazar has been banished to a bottle at the bottom of the sea, and this is my gran. Gran, this is my friend Adeel.'

'Lovely to meet you,' said Gran, who had woken up. 'But I don't see how you're going to get us out of here.'

'I'm going to wish these bars away,' said Adeel. 'Then we're going to make our escape on the magic carpets.'

'You can't!' said Jamie. 'Dakhil's lined the walls with thunderclouds. Wishes won't work in here.'

'Wishes won't work in there,' agreed Adeel, 'but they'll work just fine out here.'

'I always knew you were a smart one!' said Jamie.

Jamie and Gran watched Adeel breathe in deeply and blow out a shimmering wish. As the wish surrounded the bars, they began to disappear.

'Quick!' hissed Adeel. 'Wishes like this don't last forever! Come on!'

The window was just about big enough for Jamie and his gran to squeeze through one at a time, and clamber on to Threadbare's back. Jamie manoeuvred himself into the riding position he had perfected over weeks of practice on the magic carpet track, ruffled Threadbare's wool with a friendly hand and gripped the front two tassels like handlebars. Behind him Gran clutched his shoulders.

'We'd better get going,' said Adeel, 'before they spot that you've gone. And that this has gone too!'

Adeel lifted a cloth and revealed a battered old book with a shiny new cover. Jamie gasped. It was the Book of Wishes.

'How on Earth . . .?' said Jamie.

'There were guards in the middle tower room morning, noon and night,' he explained. 'I realised they must be guarding something. It wasn't you, so I reckoned it must be something very important. Then I saw a huge book on the table – it wasn't difficult to guess it was the Book of Wishes. I suddenly realised you must have tried to steal it. The guards were fearsome brutes with an equally fearsome appetite, and one of my jobs was to bring them sandwiches every night. This evening I put a little something extra in there: sleeping powder. They dozed off, I took the book and then came to fetch you.'

'You're a genius, Adeel!' Jamie said.

'I know.' Adeel grinned. 'And modest too!'

But just then they heard a noise behind them. Flying towards them on their own fierce magic carpets were Dakhil and Dabir, accompanied by three guards.

'Oh no!' said Adeel, kicking Sunray into action. 'We need to get out of here!'

Adeel soared into the sky and Jamie gave Threadbare's tassels a tug.

'We're right behind you!' he called as his gran held on tight. Despite the danger, Jamie couldn't help feel the thrill of being on a magic carpet once again. And he wasn't the only one.

'*Wheee!*' called Gran as Threadbare reared up after Adeel and Sunray.

The two carpets zipped into the clouds, but Dakhil and his cronies were gaining fast. Jamie stole a glance over his shoulder. Dakhil was riding the largest carpet Jamie had ever seen. It was black and embroidered in gold thread. Dabir was riding Viper, one of the fastest carpets in the Academy.

'Catch them!' bellowed Dakhil as they flew above the clouds. The guards overtook Dakhil and Dabir and sped towards Sunray and Threadbare.

'Head for Lampville,' called Adeel. 'I'm going to try and shake off these three.'

Before Jamie had time to argue, Adeel gritted his teeth, held on tight and pulled into a twisting skid, then zoomed straight towards the three guards, zipping through the clouds like lightning. When the guards realised that Adeel was going to crash into them, they panicked, yanking their

carpets to
the left and
right, but
they were too
slow. Adeel ploughed
straight through them,
scattering them like
skittles. They struggled
to keep their
balance, before falling from their carpets like
stones and landing on the soft cloud ground with
a thud.

Meanwhile, Jamie was speeding towards the

lights of Lampville. He leant forward into an aerodynamic crouch and so did Gran.

Jamie glanced round and saw that Dakhil and Dabir were still in pursuit — and getting closer. They had a carpet each while Threadbare was struggling under the weight of two riders.

'Come on, boy,' encouraged Jamie. 'You're doing great!' But it was obvious that Threadbare was tiring. If Dakhil and Dabir pulled up on either side, they would be trapped.

'Give yourself up now and I'll go easy on you,' bellowed Dakhil from behind.

High above them, Adeel shouted, 'Don't you want this, Dakhil?'

Jamie looked up to see Adeel waving the Book of Wishes in the air.

'You get the humans,' Dakhil shouted to Dabir. 'I'll get the book!'

Adeel's tactic had worked! Dabir sped after Gran and Jamie while Dakhil pulled up into the sky to chase Adeel.

Gran turned and blew a raspberry at the pursuing genie. 'Catch us if you can!' she cried, leaning forward and nudging Jamie out of the way. 'Let's see if I've still got the skills! If we can't outrun him, we'll just have to outmanoeuvre him! Time for a few tricks!'

They had reached Lampville city now, and she guided Threadbare down to street level. Gran steered like a racing pro. They dodged under washing lines and twisted between tree branches – Jamie was very impressed! She gripped the tassels hard and nudged the carpet past Lampville Jail towards the Grand Bazaar. Dabir was a good racer too, though, and wasn't left behind for long. Soon he was close enough to try to grab one of Threadbare's tassels. Jamie kicked him away with his leg, but he was quickly back on their tail.

Gran hurtled into the Grand Bazaar and zig-zagged through the stalls. Dabir and Viper struggled to manoeuvre as well as them. Gran made a last-second dodge around a stall selling pots and pans and heard a loud crash as Dabir and Viper ploughed straight through it. When Viper emerged from the other side, Dabir was wearing a saucepan on his head.

'You look like a DIY dalek!' called Jamie.

Gran laughed. 'Magic carpet racing Academy champion three years running, don't you know!'

Dabir whipped the saucepan away and continued the chase.

Up above, Adeel was more than a match for Dakhil. Dakhil's carpet was built for parades, not races. It might have been big and scary but Sunray was nimble and quick. Adeel had a bird's eye view of Jamie and watched as Gran banked hard, guiding Threadbare down a back alley. Dabir stopped following for a moment. He wasn't sure which way Jamie and his gran had gone.

Adeel saw his chance. He zoomed down, disappearing into a large fluffy cloud. Dakhil roared and gave chase. Adeel quickly switched direction inside the cloud, and sped towards Jamie and the back alley. By the time Dakhil got through, Adeel was gone.

Adeel pulled up beside Threadbare, grinning, but saw that Jamie had gone pale, and looked ahead to see why.

The alley was a dead end.

They tried to shrink into the shadows, but it

wasn't enough. Dabir and Viper came into sight, with Dakhil just behind. The friends were right against the wall and if they made a move, they would be spotted. They kept as still as statues hoping they wouldn't be seen.

Behind them a voice hissed in the darkness. 'Keep quiet or you're dead.'

Arms stretched out from the shadows and pulled them backwards into a darkened room.

CHAPTER 14

When Jamie's eyes adjusted to the light, he saw that they had been dragged into a cluttered storeroom. Gran had landed on a pile of black cloth and Adeel had tumbled face first into a basket of buttons.

'Who's there?' said Jamie angrily, rising to his feet.

'Well, you could show a bit of gratitude! I just saved you from another visit to Lampville Jail,' came a female voice.

'Ivana!' cried Jamie, giving the seamstress a warm hug.

'Shh!' said Ivana. 'That doorway is well hidden, but we can't throw a celebration disco.'

Leaving Threadbare and Sunray in the storeroom, Ivana led Jamie, Adeel and Gran into the front of her shop and pulled down the shutters. Fadiyah jumped up from her sewing machine and ushered them into comfy-looking cloud chairs.

'You seemed to be in a bit of trouble,' said Ivana as she wished up five mugs of steaming hot mint tea.

Jamie told them all about Adeel's daring rescue and the pursuit through the clouds. Then he introduced her to Gran.

'We've met before,' said Gran with a smile. 'It was a long time ago – back when I was known as Ameerah.'

Fadiyah dropped the tray of tea in shock. 'Ameerah!' she gasped.

Ivana and Fadiyah ran over and took Gran's

hands in theirs. Together they hugged and gave each other a secret handshake that looked more like a funky dance move than a greeting.

'The GGGs – together again at last!' announced Ivana triumphantly.

'That's the Girlie Genie Gang!' explained Gran to a bewildered Adeel and Jamie. 'We were at the Academy together!'

'Oh the stories I could tell . . .' said Ivana. 'Do you remember the time we wished stinky Shunnah's farts bright blue?'

Gran laughed. 'What about the time we sneaked out of art class to practise doing loop the loops on our magic carpets?'

'Is that possible?' asked Adeel.

Ivana, Fadiyah and Gran shared a mischievous look and then shook their heads.

'No!' said Fadiyah, collapsing into a fit of giggles. 'The lump on my bottom was there for six months! We tried to see you before you became a human Ameerah . . .'

'But our parents stopped us,' interrupted Ivana.

'You don't have to apologise,' said Gran with a

sympathetic smile. 'I always knew you'd have said goodbye if you could.'

While they continued reminiscing, Adeel took out the Book of Wishes.

As soon as Ivana and Fadiyah saw what he was holding they stopped laughing. 'Is that what I think it is?' asked Ivana.

'I need to wish myself back to being a genie,' Gran explained. 'Then I'm going to tackle Dakhil with a truth wish and get my brother out of jail.'

Ivana gave Gran a squeeze on the shoulder. 'You can all stay with us as long as you like. There are plenty of places to hide in my shop should anyone come snooping. Not that anyone will – there's no reason to suspect us of anything!'

'I need to rescue Balthazar too,' Jamie said. 'I

can't stand to think of him trapped in a bottle under the sea while we're all free in Lampville.'

'There'll be time for that when we've defeated Dakhil,' said Gran. 'The most important thing is saving Methuzular and the genie world!'

Jamie knew it would be better to wait, but he also knew how scared Balthazar had been of the dreaded bottle at the bottom of the sea.

Gran looked at Jamie. She could see how much Balthazar meant to him. She couldn't make him wait if he felt so strongly. So finally it was agreed that Ivana and Gran would stay and help Gran rediscover her powers. The wish to turn yourself back into a genie was a difficult one and Gran would need all the help she could get. While they practised, Adeel and Jamie would begin the hunt for Balthazar.

The next morning, Jamie and Adeel got on Sunray – Threadbare was still too tired after the chase the day before and one magic carpet was more discreet than two anyway. They realised that Dabir, as the genie who'd finally banished Balthazar, was the only person who could lead them to him and so they flew to the Academy.

As they soared high above the clouds, Adeel told Jamie that Dabir had been disappearing from lessons at odd times for a couple of days. The teachers had to let him go as his dad was the bossy headmaster and he was the even bossier head boy.

'If I know Dabir like I think I do,' said Adeel, 'I bet he's been going to tease Balthazar in the bottle. He's not the sort of genie to leave you alone when he's got you trapped. He likes to rub your nose in it.'

'That's exactly what he planned to do to me when he trapped me in a lamp,' agreed Jamie. 'If your hunch is right, we can follow him next time he goes to visit!' said Jamie.

'Exactly!' said Adeel. 'The Portal of Dreams would be the easiest way for him to go so we just need to keep an eye on the portal.'

Adeel landed Sunray behind a cloud tree and they dodged from bush to bush towards Farah's classroom and the Portal of Dreams.

Eventually they were right outside the window

to the classroom. 'If we're right, Dabir will be here at some point,' said Adeel.

The two boys climbed into the leafy branches of a nearby tree and waited. And waited. And waited.

'Maybe we were wrong about the portal. Maybe he goes a different way,' said Jamie after an hour. 'We'll just have to go inside the Academy and confront him. I know it'll be dangerous, but we've got to rescue Balthazar.'

Just then, they saw the door opening. Dabir was sneaking inside Farah's classroom.

From the safety of the cloud tree, Jamie and Adeel watched Dabir wheel the portal into the middle of the classroom. They climbed around the tree, balancing on a branch so they could see where Dabir was going.

They watched Dabir guide the image on the screen with quick flicks of his wrist. The Earth appeared on the screen.

'At least he's on this planet!' said Adeel with a smile.

As the image of the Earth spun on

the portal, they realised just how much of it was made of water. Dabir was guiding the image towards what Jamie recognised as Australia. There was some point to geography lessons after all! When the picture came to rest, Jamie could see bright blue flowers and tall palm trees on the screen.

Dabir rubbed his hands together and stepped through.

Jamie and Adeel quickly clambered down from the tree. Adeel wished the window lock open and they squeezed inside. Through the portal, they watched Dabir turn himself into a glittering silver fish and plunge into the waves.

'He's using a transformation wish,' explained Adeel. 'We'll have to do the same if we're going to find Balthazar!'

Jamie was just about to remind Adeel that he didn't know the transformation wish – it was far too advanced for him. Adeel had obviously forgotten Jamie had only spent one term in the Academy. But before he could say anything, his friend had hopped through the screen and was gone.

Jamie felt the tingle in his tummy as he followed him through the portal, and arrived on a hot, sandy, deserted beach. Dabir had obviously picked somewhere where he could come and go unseen to make taunting Balthazar easier. The waves crashed in the distance and Jamie and Adeel breathed in deep lungfuls of fresh sea air as they quickly took cover behind a large palm tree.

After a few minutes, a big silver fish leapt from the surf. Jamie gasped in amazement as it transformed, mid-air, back into the shape of Dabir. He landed in the sand with a soft thud and grinned. The fact that Dabir had obviously enjoyed mocking Balthazar so much made Jamie furious.

Once Dabir had returned through the portal, Jamie and Adeel ran towards the shore. Jamie stole a look at the shimmering image of Farah's classroom.

'What if he guides the portal away from us?' said Jamie as they ran.

'He's the only one that uses the portal these days,' said Adeel. 'I doubt he bothers to reset it when he's finished – why would he? All the same, we'd better be quick. Come on, let's transform ourselves into fish!'

'But I haven't learnt that yet,' said Jamie.

Adeel looked thoughtful. 'I can't wish for both of us,' he said. 'It would wear me out and I'd have no energy left to swim. I'm still only a trainee, remember. How about using the attribute wish you learnt last term? If you can't transform yourself into a fish, wishing you could breathe like a fish would be the next best thing. You go first, and I'll copy you.'

Of course! Why hadn't he thought of that? Jamie closed his eyes and breathed deeply. He took his mind to the special place where magic could happen and concentrated as hard as he could,

changing the words of the attribute wish to guide his mind for what he needed.

> '*Shimmering scales and flashing fin,*
> *Let my alteration begin.*
> *Hear my call and hear my wish,*
> *Let me breathe just like a fish.*'

Jamie felt the click in the back of his mind that told him his wish could be granted and blew out a sparkling breath of air. The wish enveloped him and he ran into the waves. As he dived under the surf he took a breath – and found he could breathe under the sea just as easily as he did on land!

Above him there was a splash and Adeel plunged down to join him. Together they swam past craggy black rocks and brightly coloured fish. They scoured the ocean floor, but there were hundreds of nooks and crannies in between the starfish-strewn rocks and coral. If it wasn't for the fact that his poor friend was in trouble, Jamie would have enjoyed it, even though they had to dive and twist to avoid jellyfish and slithering eels.

Finally something shiny caught his eye. A bottle glinted in the sunlight, wedged between two rocks in a clump of seaweed!

Jamie dived down, feeling very relieved – but it was just an empty pop bottle that someone had thrown away.

Then he spotted something sparkling over by a jagged rock. It certainly looked like the bottle he had last seen on Dakhil's desk in Alim Tower. As he got close, he could see the glum figure of Balthazar Najar inside.

Balthazar jumped when he saw Jamie's massive face. Jamie scooped up the bottle and swam for the surface. As Jamie and Adeel bobbed in the waves, they gave each other a high five. But Adeel's face turned pale, and he pointed over his friend's shoulder.

A big black fin had broken through the waves and was swimming straight for them!

Adeel and Jamie swam as fast as they could. Jamie looked over his shoulder and saw the flashing white teeth of a great white shark bearing down on him. Adeel had made it back to the beach and stood shouting at his friend – but Jamie was trying to swim with only one hand, because the other was clutching the bottle.

Jamie heard the swish of the shark's powerful tail and smelt the stink of rotten fish from its terrifying jaws. He felt the rush of water rising behind him as the shark prepared to attack. In desperation, Jamie threw Balthazar's bottle to Adeel. 'You can still save Lampville!' he shouted as he saw the shark's glinting teeth in the corner of his eye.

Then Jamie saw a cloud of sparkles coming towards him and the shark.

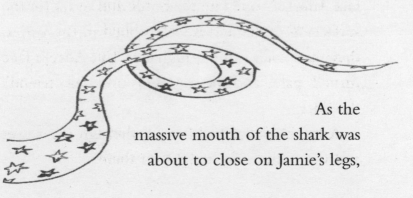

As the massive mouth of the shark was about to close on Jamie's legs, it suddenly froze. The shark turned bright purple and shot out of the water and flew towards the horizon like a deflating balloon. A startled seagull dived out of the way as the shark shot past and landed with a splash far out to sea.

'What did you do?' Jamie asked Adeel, paddling towards shore.

'I gave him the wind power of a trumping baby!' wheezed an exhausted Adeel. 'Just for a couple of seconds. But that really took it out of me!'

Jamie shook himself dry. That had been close! 'I owe you one,' he said. 'Your magic's got even more amazing since I've been away. Now let's get Balthazar out of this bottle.'

'We need a human for that,' said Adeel.

'I'll do it,' Jamie said, preparing to rub.

'You can't release the same genie twice. It won't work. We need someone else.'

'What? Why didn't you tell me that before?' Jamie said.

'I thought everybody knew that,' said Adeel. 'It stops one person getting too many wishes.'

Jamie kicked the sand in frustration. He'd nearly been eaten by a shark – and it was all for nothing.

'You must know loads of humans,' said Adeel. 'Surely one of them should be able to help.'

Jamie thought for a moment and then smiled. 'I know just the person,' he said.

CHAPTER 15

Jamie and Adeel dived back through the portal into the darkness of Farah's empty classroom. Then Jamie carefully manipulated the portal back towards his school. It was now breaktime there and he could see his friends playing football. Dylan was dribbling the ball towards a makeshift goal.

'That's my best friend,' he explained. 'Best *human* friend, that is,' added Jamie quickly – he didn't want to hurt Adeel's feelings. 'He'll help us.'

Jamie grabbed Adeel's hand and together they stepped through the portal into the human world.

Dylan was just about to shoot when he saw Jamie dressed in very peculiar clothes with a boy with pointy ears, both waving at him from behind a tree. Distracted, he fired the shot well wide of the goal and earned a slow handclap from his team-mates.

'Well done, blunder boot!' someone shouted. 'You have to go and fetch that now!'

Dylan scurried after the ball, threw it back, and told his friends to play on without him – he wanted to see what Jamie was up to.

'Where have you been?!' said Dylan. 'The last time I saw you, you disappeared into a toilet!'

'This is Adeel,' explained Jamie. 'Adeel, this is Dylan. I'll tell you everything just as soon as I can, Dylan, but first we need your help. The future of the genie world depends on it.'

Dylan beamed. 'I always knew I was destined for greatness!'

'Rub this,' said Jamie, giving him the bottle.

Dylan's face fell. 'Is that all?' he said. 'No kung-fu? I can do a mean Chinese burn, you know.'

Jamie and Adeel shook their heads and Dylan rubbed the bottle with the sleeve of his jumper.

Nothing happened.

Dylan rubbed harder and the bottle began to quiver and shake in his hands. He dropped it in surprise and it landed on the grass with a dull thud and began to spin round and round. The cork flew out of the end and bright red smoke billowed from its neck. There was a strange whistle and a loud pop and then Jamie heard a familiar giggle.

'Hee! Hee! Heeeeeeeeeeeeee!' said Balthazar as he flew from the bottle. 'Free at last! Now I know how lemonade feels!' He somersaulted to the ground. Balthazar threw his arms over Jamie and Adeel's shoulders.

'Thanks you two for coming to find me! It was terrible.' Balthazar wrung his hands. 'Honestly! If I

ever see another seahorse it'll be too soon. But I'm forgetting something!' Balthazar grabbed Dylan by the arm and spun him round. 'Thank you, human. You've set me free – which means you get three wishes.'

Jamie pushed Balthazar towards the portal.

'They'll have to wait. We need to get back. Someone could move the portal at any time.' He turned back to Dylan. 'Thanks so much for helping – we'll be back really soon . . . I hope.'

Dylan stared with wide eyes as they all stepped through into a strange-looking classroom, and then vanished.

Back at the Academy, Jamie and his two genie friends hurried to the window and ran to where Sunray was waiting for them. Sunray was pleased to see them and smothered them all in a clothy cuddle.

'Reckon you can take three?' asked Jamie.

Sunray flicked his tassels in reply and they clambered aboard.

They all held tight as Sunray soared over the gates of the Academy towards Lampville. With his friends beside him, Jamie felt ready to confront Dakhil and Dabir.

CHAPTER 16

Evening was falling and far below Jamie could see the lamplighters making their way through the streets of the city, lighting flaming torches to keep the shadows at bay.

As they soared over the Grand Bazaar, Adeel tapped Jamie on the shoulder and pointed. A crowd of genies had gathered in the middle of the square and Dakhil was addressing them, punching his fist to emphasise what he was saying.

Jamie landed Sunray on a nearby building and guided him behind a chimney pot so that they could listen without being seen.

'The humans have stolen our Book of Wishes,' shouted Dakhil. He clapped his hands and the guards that had chased them on their magic carpets the day before made their way onto the podium and told everyone that it was true. 'The sister of the traitor Methuzular, the only genie to have wished herself human, has betrayed us all and is helping them as I speak!'

A cry of shock came from the crowd.

'Do not fear!' said Dakhil, calming them with his hands. 'For weeks I suspected the humans might try something like this, which is why I have trained a genie army to defend Lampville in case they attacked. But this is no longer enough! They have declared war by stealing the Book of Wishes. Now we must take the fight to them! I am going to Cloud Hall to speak to the rest of the Genie Congress and seek permission to attack the human world! We have worked tirelessly for the humans without thanks,' continued Dakhil. 'It is time they worked for us.'

The crowd cheered as one, and Jamie felt sick. How could Dakhil mislead them all like that? 'When those genies know that everything Dakhil is saying is a lie they won't be so keen,' said Jamie, steering Sunray back to Ivana's shop.

But although Gran, Fadiyah and Ivana welcomed them back and were thrilled to see Balthazar again, something was obviously wrong. Gran was sitting in a cloud chair with the Book of Wishes open on her lap, frowning deeply.

'It's no use, Jamie,' she said quietly. 'I can't turn myself back.'

Jamie ran to his grandmother's side and squeezed her shoulder gently. 'I'm sure if you try again, Gran . . .' he began.

'We've been trying ever since you left,' said Ivana, slumping down next to her. 'Nothing's worked. Even though she is now a human, Ameerah should have enough magic left in her to make this wish, but she has obviously been a human for too long – she can't remember how to make wishes.'

'Dakhil is on his way to the Congress to get permission to lead an attack on the humans,' said Balthazar. 'You've got to do it now!'

Adeel studied the wish on the page and ran his finger across the words. 'What if we all try?' he said thoughtfully. 'When something's difficult in class, we practise a wish together before trying it on our own. We combine our genie magic to make it easier for the person who then makes the wish.'

'It's worth a try,' said Gran.

Ivana cleared a space in the centre of the room. Then Gran sat down in the middle and the others all sat in a circle around her holding hands.

'We say the wish together,' explained Adeel. 'Then we all blow our wishes towards Ameerah as she says the wish for herself. Our combined magic might just give her the power to turn herself back into a genie.'

They all closed their eyes to help them concentrate. Ivana told them the words that would help take their minds to that special place where magic might happen.

'*May she live lightly,*
May she shine brightly,
May she be a genie once more.
Bring a point to each ear,
Make her wishes ring clear,
Make her the genie she was before!'

They began to chant the words quietly and Jamie felt himself getting lost in the rhythm. His mind cleared of all other thoughts – of stopping

Dakhil, of freeing Methuzular — and, powered by those magical words, he felt transported to a place where anything was possible. When Ivana stopped chanting, they opened their eyes and exchanged a look. It felt as if they were all charged with electricity. Together they inhaled deeply, as if sucking all the air from the room. Then they looked at Gran and breathed out a shimmering, sparkling wish, brighter than any Jamie had seen before. The four clouds of sparkles hovered in the air, and then began to dance together, shrouding Gran with their power.

Jamie held his breath as Gran disappeared in a cloud of golden stars as she then said the wish once more. When the fog lifted, they let go of each others' hands and stared.

Gran's skin seemed to shine a little brighter and her eyes twinkled with mysterious power. Gran's ears had always been pointy, but they seemed to become even pointier.

'I think it's worked,' she whispered. 'I feel magic running through my veins. My bones don't ache and I don't think I need these any more!' She whipped off her glasses.

'I can see perfectly!' Gran jumped to her feet and breathed in deeply. She blew out a sparkly wish and an explosion of confetti erupted over the room.

Ivana rummaged in a chest at the back of the shop and pulled out some red Najar robes and five brightly coloured waistcoats. 'Let's show Dakhil we don't like his ideas.'

Gran got changed into the flowing robes behind a curtain and came out looking every inch the genie she now was.

The other genies swapped their black waistcoats for the colourful ones Ivana had found. Balthazar and Jamie changed into Najar red to match Ameerah, Adeel wore Maloof yellow, and Ivana and Fadiyah wore multi-coloured waistcoats Ivana had made. 'Our grandparents were all of different clans, so I don't see why we shouldn't wear all the colours,' Ivana announced. 'Come on – let's go and make Dakhil tell the truth.'

'You remember the wish?' checked Jamie as he and Gran jumped aboard Threadbare. 'Otherwise we could take the Book of Wishes with us.'

Gran shook her head. 'The book is safest hidden here until we can place it into Methuzular's hands ourselves. We spent so long practising the wish in Alim Tower I'm never going to forget it!'

She tugged on Threadbare's tassels and Jamie held on tight. Behind them Ivana, Fadiyah, Balthazar and Adeel clambered onto Sunray and together they took off into the night. Jamie wished he could be as excited as his friends as they raced towards Cloud Hall, but as it loomed into view he couldn't help but feel the most dangerous part of their mission was only just beginning.

CHAPTER 17

Cloud Hall was a magnificent building. Every part was covered in ornate carvings, and imposing statues of famous genies peered down at Gran and Jamie as they hopped off Threadbare and marched through the arched doorway. Jamie realised that, for the first time since he had returned to Lampville, he was not trying to creep around, but instead was walking proudly.

Nobody was allowed into the main chamber of

Cloud Hall unless they were a member of the Genie Congress or had business with them and so Dakhil's guards were lounging in chairs outside the doors. Jamie could hear Dakhil's booming voice echoing from within as he spoke to the other members of the Genie Congress. They didn't have a second to lose.

Just then, one of the guards spotted Jamie and his friends. He jumped to his feet and pointed, alerting the other guards and they all rushed towards them. Ivana, Fadiyah and Gran shared a look.

'The GGG special?' said Ivana.

Fadiyah and Gran nodded and together they blew a wish at the guards. Jamie watched as the sparkling clouds shimmered all around them and then heard five thuds as the guards fell to the floor. 'What did you do?' asked Balthazar. 'The GGG special is a sleeping wish,' explained

Gran. 'We used to do it when we needed to sneak out of lessons. Only in dire emergencies, of course.'

'When they wake up, they won't remember a thing,' said Fadiyah.

Gran adjusted her robes in a mirror that was twice as tall as her and nodded to them all. 'Ready?'

Adeel and Jamie stood at Gran's left shoulder while Balthazar, Ivana and Fadiyah flanked her right. Then Gran flung open the doors to Cloud Hall and they all stormed inside.

The Genie Congress was made up of ten genies clad in regal gold outfits. They were sitting around a grand cloud table. All of them looked up when Gran made her entrance.

'What is the meaning of this?' blustered an old genie with a long grey beard. 'As vice president of the Genie Congress, I demand to be told!'

Dakhil, who was standing at a lectern with Dabir by his side, was shocked to see Balthazar free, but quickly pointed to all of them. 'These are the traitors I was telling you about!' he shouted. 'They stole the Book of Wishes. The human boy is Methuzular's spy who infiltrated the Academy last year, and the old woman is the traitor Ameerah who turned her back on the genie world and wished herself human.'

The members of the Genie Congress gasped as they began to recognise the powerful genie who had left them all those years ago.

'It's true,' said Gran. 'I am Ameerah Najar, Methuzular's sister – but I am no traitor and I am now a genie again, like you. I have returned to put right the damage Dakhil has done.'

The vice president rose to his feet and took a step towards Ameerah. He stroked his beard flat against his chest and shook his head. 'I was here the day you asked to become a human,' he said. 'You were told never to return.'

'I remember. You're Saba, aren't you?' said Gran. 'You never said a harsh word to me when I chose to leave. You seemed to respect my choice.'

Saba narrowed his eyes. 'Be that as it may, you shouldn't have come back. Your brother is a traitor. We've seen the letter, we know all about the plan!'

'There *is* no plan, Saba,' said Gran. 'Dakhil

tricked you. He made my brother write that letter and then locked him away in Lampville Jail. Balthazar here will tell you what happened, and Jamie saw Methuzular in the prison.'

'It's lies! All lies!' spluttered Dakhil hitting the lectern in anger. 'She would say that! And we all know that Balthazar is *always* getting things wrong.'

Saba held up his hand for quiet. 'Ameerah was many things,' said Saba, 'but I never believed she was a traitor. Ameerah's only crime was to fall in love.'

'She's a traitor just like her brother,' spat Dakhil. 'She chose the human world over ours. She can't be trusted!'

'It is you who can't be trusted,' said Gran. 'You have been looking for an excuse to wreak revenge on the human world ever since your cowardly father disappeared!'

A second gasp echoed around the chamber. They all knew the story but no one had dared speak of it since Dakhil came to power.

'You are an old woman,' Dakhil said. 'You do

not know what you are saying. That mouth of yours should be kept shut. Permanently.'

Dakhil drew breath and blew a wish at Gran. Gran tried to dodge out of the way but the sparkling cloud followed and danced around her. When it had disappeared everyone looked on in horror – Gran's mouth had completely disappeared!

Jamie suddenly realised how serious the situation was. Their plan was for Gran to cast the truth wish on Dakhil so he had to admit to what he had done. How could she do that without a mouth?!

But Gran held up a hand. She breathed out through her nose and wished her mouth back exactly as it had been.

'Wow! It's really difficult to reverse a wish like that, especially a wish that has been cast by a genie as powerful as Dakhil,' whispered Adeel to Jamie. 'It will make the Congress listen to her.'

'Is that the best you can do?' she said. 'You really should learn to keep your hair on, Dakhil!' And with that, Gran blew a wish at him. As it shrouded his head, Dakhil's hair began to grow and grow. It looped itself around his neck and chest like rope.

Dakhil's arms were clamped to his side as if he were wearing a very hairy straitjacket.

'Enough!' ordered Saba. 'This is no way to solve things!'

But Dakhil was in no mood to stop now. He wished his hair back to normal and then stared angrily at Gran. 'Shouldn't you be at home in a rocking chair?' he spat.

A rocking chair appeared behind Gran and scooped her up. Ropes came from the chair's arms and held her in place. The chair began to rock back and forth, gently at first but getting faster and faster by the second, until it bucked like a thrill ride at a fun fair. Gran's face was a blur.

Suddenly the chair stopped rocking and the

ropes dissolved in a shower of stars. Gran grinned at Dakhil and his laughter stuck in his throat.

'Thanks, Dakhil,' said Gran. 'I enjoyed that. This old lady still likes to rock and roll.'

The chair swung back one last time and catapulted Gran out like a bowling ball. She rocketed towards Dakhil, knocking him off his feet and sending him tumbling to the floor.

Dakhil roared, leaping to his feet, and Gran turned just in time to dodge out of his way, but Dakhil wasn't finished. He flew upwards and rained down bolts of lightning at Gran's feet as the rest of the Genie Congress hid under their long table.

Jamie's mouth hung open in disbelief. These
wishes were more powerful than any he had ever
seen — or even heard about. Gran dodged the
lightning bolts and began to spin like a human
tornado. She leapt into the air and soon Dakhil
and Gran were lost in a flurry of lightning bolts
and wish clouds.

The pair of genies hit the ceiling, breaking
through as a clump of cloud fell to the floor and
evaporated into dust. Jamie watched, eyes wide, as
Gran and Dakhil spun across the sky, their wishes
flying around them in a blaze. Suddenly there was

a massive flash of light and Gran and Dakhil plummeted to the floor, landing in a plume of shimmering smoke. Dakhil pulled himself up but Gran lay exactly where she had fallen.

'Gran!' cried Jamie, running to her side.

She smiled weakly as Jamie cradled her in his arms. She was too exhausted even to stand. Dakhil towered over them, menace glinting in his eyes.

'Surrender,' he sneered. 'You are defeated.'

Gran looked up from the floor and shook her head. 'Never! You are a liar and a cheat,' she said.

'You are the liar,' said Dakhil.

'I just wish I knew who was telling the truth!' cried Saba in frustration.

Jamie suddenly remembered. Of course! The truth wish! Now was the time to use it. In all the excitement, they'd forgotten all about it. 'Go on, Gran,' he whispered. 'Make the wish.'

'I can't, Jamie,' she said. 'I'm exhausted.'

Suddenly Jamie heard Methuzular's voice in his head. It was repeating the wish over and over again. He remembered helping Gran practise the wish when they were in the tower.

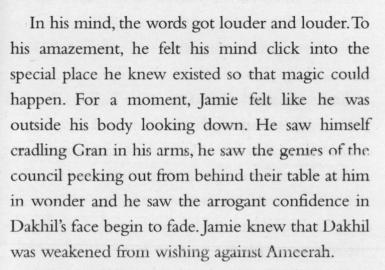

'May this genie now be honest and true,
May his lies disappear like morning dew.
May he speak free from deceit and fuss
And may he tell only the truth to us.'

In his mind, the words got louder and louder. To his amazement, he felt his mind click into the special place he knew existed so that magic could happen. For a moment, Jamie felt like he was outside his body looking down. He saw himself cradling Gran in his arms, he saw the genies of the council peeking out from behind their table at him in wonder and he saw the arrogant confidence in Dakhil's face begin to fade. Jamie knew that Dakhil was weakened from wishing against Ameerah.

Jamie looked up at his friends. Balthazar gave him a double thumbs-up.

It was all the encouragement he needed. He repeated the words out loud. Then he drew a deep, deep breath, and held it just for a moment before blowing a cloud of shimmering stars and sparkles towards Dakhil. Dakhil was backing away, but the wish was too fast and powerful to dodge.

'A truth wish!' gasped Saba as the cloud enveloped Dakhil.

The sparkling air disappeared and Dakhil stood there looking shocked.

'How on cloud did you do that?' gasped Adeel, looking at Jamie in admiration.

'It was like Methuzular was with me,' said Jamie. 'Helping me with his voice.'

'Rubbish,' said Balthazar with a grin. 'You're just a genie genius! I always knew you were.'

Saba was the first of the Genie Congress to gather his senses. 'Do you promise to tell the truth?' he asked Dakhil in a loud, clear voice.

Dakhil tried to hold his head steady, but despite himself, he nodded.

'Well, let's find out,' said Balthazar with a mischievous smile. 'What colour underpants are you wearing?'

Dakhil's eyes grew wide. 'Red spotty ones,' he blurted, pulling down just enough of his pantaloons so that everyone could see. Then he clamped his hands to his mouth trying to force the words back in.

Balthazar was on a roll. 'How many times a day do you fart?' he asked.

'About fifteen,' admitted Dakhil. 'More on Sundays because I have cloud stew!'

Dakhil's cheeks burnt bright red with embarrassment and Dabir hid his head in his hands.

'Enough of this!' said Saba. 'We have serious questions.' He glared at Dakhil. 'Is it true that you have lied to the Genie Congress?'

Dakhil couldn't help but nod.

'Is it true that rather than going away, Methuzular is locked up in prison, and you made him write that letter?'

'I did!' cried Dakhil. 'I made it all up. Dabir even helped with some of it!'

'Dad!' spluttered Dabir.

'Sorry, son,' said Dakhil. 'But you did.'

The vice president looked at Dakhil in disbelief. 'And what about the humans?' he asked. 'Are they really planning to turn genies into slaves?'

Dakhil shook his head. 'They know nothing about us. I'm just sick and tired of giving wishes away for free. They don't deserve our help after what happened to my father. It's their fault he was banished, asking for tricky wishes all the time!' Dakhil crumpled to the floor and hung his head in shame.

The vice president took a step towards him, anger blazing in his eyes. 'Dakhil Ganim!' he growled. 'In all my years as a genie I have never known such deceit. You, and Dabir, have abused the trust of every genie, and you must both be punished.'

The Congress huddled together for a moment and Jamie tried to listen in to their hushed discussion. When they had finished, the vice president looked at Dakhil and Dabir.

'Because you have both broken the Genie Code many times over,' he said, 'you shall be banished to a bottle at the bottom of the sea.'

Dakhil and Dabir looked to the floor in horror.

'There you must think about what you have done,' the vice president said, clicking his fingers and a bottle appeared at his feet.

'Just the one?' whispered Dabir uncertainly.

'It'll be a little bit cramped, but we thought you'd like to keep each other company,' said Saba.

'But he snores!' shouted Dabir.

The vice president blew a sparkling wish towards them, the two genies shrunk to the size of fleas and together they tumbled down into the bottle.

'Give my love to the seahorses!' called Balthazar as the bottle disappeared.

CHAPTER 18

Word spread quickly through Lampville that Dakhil had been banished – and why. Genies gathered in the Grand Bazaar to discuss what had happened. They were horrified by what Dakhil had done. Many said they had never trusted him in the first place, and that they actually quite liked humans, but hadn't dared admit it to each other because of all the guards and spies – they'd all been afraid they'd end up in Lampville Jail. They vowed never to let fear like that affect their judgement again. Every genie changed back into their clan waistcoats and colour returned to the town once more.

Jamie and his gran were asked to stand on a platform in the centre of the square and speak to the assembled genies. Jamie was a bit nervous, but he wanted to put the record straight.

'Humans don't want you to be their pets!' he told them all. 'Most humans don't even know that you exist. You watch the human world from on high, and help us when you can. When something goes our way, or the right thing happens at exactly the right time, we put it down to good luck. That might be true some of the time, but I know that it also has a lot to do with you helping us when you can. Humans never say thank you, but how could we thank you if we don't know you exist? And yet you still help us. I want to say thank you now, on behalf of humans everywhere, for the wonderful work you do.'

Just then, a cry rang out, starting from the back of the bazaar, and building until the whole crowd

was parting. Methuzular stepped forward. Everyone was shocked to see how skinny he had become, but despite his bedraggled state, his eyes shone proudly.

Gran ran to greet her brother. She threw her arms around his neck and held him tight.

'I'm so happy you came back,' whispered Methuzular.

'It's good to see you, brother,' said Gran, standing back to look at him, 'but you could really do with a beard trim!'

After the crowd heard all they had to say, they rode back to the Academy. Word had not yet reached the pupils that Dakhil was gone and Methuzular was headmaster again.

Adeel went in first and told all the genies to make their way to the school hall.

The hall was decorated with black flags and banners. When Methuzular took to the stage, the

genies couldn't believe what they were seeing, and they began to applaud and cheer.

Methuzular calmed them with his hands. 'Dakhil is gone,' he said loudly. 'So all these horrible black banners must go too!

> '*Maloof yellow and Ganim blue,*
> *The days of black and dark are through.*
> *Kassab green and Najar red,*
> *Let us have bright banners instead!*'

Methuzular drew a breath and blew a sparkling wish. As the starry cloud travelled through the hall, it transformed the black banners into the red, blue, yellow and green they had once been.

'Lessons are going to be back to normal from now on,' said Methuzlar.

'Even carpet-repairing?' groaned a genie near the back.

Methuzlar nodded and everyone laughed.

'We have someone to thank for this,' said Methuzular, beckoning Jamie onto the stage. 'A human who was brave and strong and who was prepared to live lightly and shine brightly as every genie should.'

When Jamie's old school friends saw him on the stage they stood and cheered. He called his gran, Adeel, Balthazar, Ivana and Fadiyah to join him – he couldn't have done it without them. Together they soaked up the applause and bowed to the clapping genies.

The following morning, Fadiyah set up a stall in the hall with her sister and all the trainee genies lined up to receive brand new waistcoats in their clan colours. By the end of the day, the Academy was back to being the cheery, bright place Jamie remembered.

Jamie and his gran stayed for a few weeks in Lampville. Jamie caught up with all of his friends and brushed up on his genie magic. He joined in with classes and began to try and learn the transformation wish for himself. When he wasn't in lessons, he spent most of his time with Adeel, flying around the magic carpet track on Threadbare. Jamie also learnt some new skills. Archery and fire-breathing were a lot of fun, sword swallowing was very dangerous until Adeel explained that you didn't actually have to swallow the sword completely, and Jamie loved learning to juggle, although he wasn't quite ready for the flaming torches just yet.

Gran and Methuzular spent every evening talking together. Methuzular had been keeping an eye on his sister through the Portal of Dreams so knew much of what had happened to her, but she filled in the gaps, and Gran learnt how her brother had come to be headmaster. He even let her know some of the secrets contained in the Book of Wishes.

When word spread that Ameerah was back, genies travelled from far and wide to visit their old friend and on their final night, the Academy held a banquet in Jamie and Gran's honour. Adeel wished up some delicious fig burgers and Jamie wished everyone a massive bowl of his legendary ice cream sundae.

After the banquet, Methuzular led Jamie and Gran to Farah's classroom and the Portal of Dreams. 'Your school day on Earth is nearly at an end,' he said softly to Jamie. 'It's time to go home.'

CHAPTER 19

Through the Portal of Dreams, Jamie watched everyone getting ready for hometime. Miss Rothwell was giving them their homework, and Jamie watched Dylan take out his robo-bugs ready for a quick game in the playground.

Methuzular gave his sister a hug. 'You don't have to go, you know,' he said. 'You can always stay and help me at the Academy.'

Gran smiled, but shook her head. Methuzular

understood. Gran's life was on Earth now. He blew a wish towards his sister and Jamie watched as her ears lost a little of their pointiness and she became human once again.

Ivana appeared at the door with Gran's old clothes and glasses. Jamie sighed and took back his school uniform.

He gave Adeel a friendly handshake. 'I'll be back to taste more of your cooking soon!' he said. Then he turned to Methuzular. 'Until the next time,' he whispered as Methuzular held him close in a hug.

Through the portal, Jamie heard the school bell ring. Balthazar patted him on the back as he put his leg through the shimmering screen. 'See you soon, genie genius.' Jamie felt his stomach tingle as they stepped back into the boys' toilets. He got changed quickly, stuffed his genie outfit back into his rucksack and then he and Gran crept into the playground. Outside, Jamie's mum was waiting for them.

'Good day at school, Mum?' she called as Gran tottered out of the gate.

'Oh yes,' said Gran, giving Jamie a smile. 'It was action-packed!'

As they turned to begin the walk home, Dylan ran after them. 'Wait!' he called. 'You've got some explaining to do, Jamie Quinn!'

Jamie let Gran and Mum walk ahead and waited while his friend caught up.

'Did I help save the genie world?'

Jamie nodded and Dylan punched the air.

'I *knew* we'd do it!' he said.

Jamie rolled his eyes and smiled. He thought that he and his gran had done more than Dylan, but he was happy to let his friend share their triumph.

Dylan and Jamie sat on a low wall and chatted away. 'So when are you going back?' he whispered. 'What's the Academy like now? You have to take me next time! They'll probably erect a statue in my honour or something!'

Before Jamie could answer there was a puff of smoke and a flash of light and a tiny Balthazar Najar hovered in front of them.

'Miss me already?' asked Jamie, grinning at the genie.

'I'm not here for you,' said Balthazar. 'I'm here for him.' Balthazar pointed at Dylan.

'M–m–me?' stammered Dylan, his eyes wide.

'Yup!' said Balthazar, doing a loop the loop. 'You freed me from the bottle so I owe you three wishes. What'll they be?'

Dylan's face broke into a broad smile. 'Wow!' he said. 'Three wishes! Brilliant! Well I've always wished I had a sausage dog . . .'

'Brilliant!' said Balthazar. 'The first thing we need is a jumbo pack of sausages!'

Dylan looked confused. 'I'm not sure that's how sausage dogs are made . . .' he said uncertainly.

But Balthazar wasn't listening, his mind was already fizzing with plans and magic.

Jamie laughed and ran to catch up with his gran. He knew that Dylan would soon learn Balthazar's magic didn't always go to plan, but he also knew his friend was in for the time of his life as he found that out for himself!

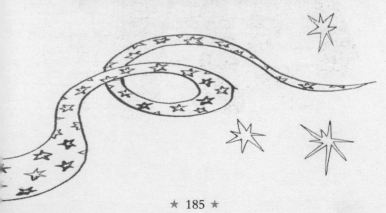

Have you read . . .

GENIE IN TRAINING

When Jamie's gran gives him a battered old
teapot he reckons she's gone doolally!
But then he cleans it, and out pops
Balthazar Najar, a banished genie!

Balthazar grants three wishes, but for the last one,
Jamie accidentally wishes he was a genie . . .
He's whisked off to genie school where
an angry headmaster, a suspiciously friendly
snake and deadly magic carpet races
are the least of his worries!

Coming soon . . .

When Balthazar and Dylan, Jamie's two best
friends, lure him back to Lampville with the
promise of a fantastic adventure, Jamie finds
himself stuck in a trap so fiendishly difficult he's
not sure he'll ever get out!

Why have his friends tricked him? Who is the
mysterious cloaked genie who seems to have
them under his spell and what terrible plan does
he have for Jamie and the Genie Academy?

In this latest hilarious adventure, Jamie will have
to escape poison spikes, fire breathing toads and
double-crossing friends to make sure the genie
world is not destroyed for ever.

Sometimes magic just isn't enough . . .

WISHING FOR MORE?

Come and explore
the Genie Academy website
for fun and games,
book news and much, much more!

GENIEACADEMY.CO.UK